By Peter Lovesey

Sergeant Cribb series
Wobble to Death
The Detective Wore Silk
Drawers
Abracadaver
Mad Hatter's Holiday
Invitation to a Dynamite Party
A Case of Spirits
Swing, Swing Together
Waxwork

Albert Edward,
Prince of Wales series
Bertie and the Tinman
Bertie and the Seven Bodies
Bertie and the Crime of
Passion

Peter Diamond series
The Last Detective
Diamond Solitaire
The Summons
Bloodhounds
Upon a Dark Night
The Vault
Diamond Dust
The House Sitter
The Secret Hangman
Skeleton Hill
Stagestruck
Cop to Corpse
The Tooth Tattoo

The Stone Wife
Down Among the Dead Men
Another One Goes Tonight
Beau Death
Killing With Confetti
The Finisher

Hen Mallin series
The Circle
The Headhunters

Other fiction
Goldengirl (as Peter Lear)
Spider Girl (as Peter Lear)
The False Inspector Dew
Keystone
Rough Cider
On the Edge
The Secret of Spandau (as
Peter Lear)
The Reaper

Short stories
Butchers and other stories of
crime
The Crime of Miss Oyster
Brown and other stories
Do Not Exceed the Stated
Dose
The Sedgemoor Strangler and
other stories of crime
Murder on the Short List

Peter Lovesey was born in Middlesex and studied at Hampton Grammar School and Reading University, where he met his wife Jax. He won a competition with his first crime fiction novel, *Wobble to Death*, and has never looked back, with his numerous books winning and being short-listed for nearly all the prizes in the international crime writing world.

He was chairman of the Crime Writers' Association and has been presented with Lifetime Achievement awards both in the UK and the US.

For more info, visit Peter's website at www.peterlovesey.com

Peter **LOVESEY**

A Case of Spirits

sphere

SPHERE

First published by Macmillan in 1975
This reissue published by Sphere in 2020

Copyright © Peter Lovesey 1975

A CIP catalogue record for this book is available from the British Library.

ISBN 978-0-7515-8112-6

Typeset in ITC New Baskerville by Palimpsest Book Production Ltd,
Falkirk, Stirlingshire
Printed and bound in Great Britain by Clays Ltd, Elcograf S.p.A

Papers used by Sphere are from well-managed forests
and other responsible sources.

MIX
Paper from
responsible sources
FSC® C104740

Sphere
An imprint of
Little, Brown Book Group
Carmelite House
50 Victoria Embankment
London EC4Y 0DZ

An Hachette UK Company
www.hachette.co.uk

www.littlebrown.co.uk

A Case of Spirits

'What's a "medium"? He's a means,
Good, bad, indifferent, still the only means
Spirits can speak by.'

'What do you take me for? It's more than my career's
worth to 'elp meself to clients' property. Jesus, I'm
booked for another three seances at Dr Probert's. Scientific
stuff. The next one's on Saturday. I'd 'ave to be off me
'ead to filch 'is pictures, wouldn't I?'

Cribb nodded. 'No question about it.' He leaned forward.
'These things that happen in the seances, Mr Brand. Spirit
hands and that sort of thing. Do you actually believe in
'em yourself?'

There was a pause. Then Brand said, 'You're tryin' to
trap me, Copper. I ain't obtainin' money by false pretences
if that's what you mean. My clients understand that I can't
guarantee nothin' without the co-operation of the spirits.
You can ask Miss Crush or Dr Probert or 'is daughter or
any of 'em what they've seen and 'eard. Things 'appen
when I put my 'ands on a table, strange things that none
of us can account for, nor control, not even them that
comes from Scotland Yard. 'Ave you ever 'eard of objects
being spirited away?'

1

'Yes, quite often,' said Thackeray, 'but we always get the blighters in the end.'

1

It's all absurd, and yet
There's something in it all, I know: how much?
No answer!

F our pairs of hands were pressed palm downwards on
the mess-room table at Paradise Street Police Station,
Rotherhithe. A uniformed sergeant, pale and gaunt behind
a magnificent moustache, was exhaling evenly and audibly,
as if at a medical inspection. But his eyes were closed, in
the proper manner of a medium in trance.

'By George, I can hear something rapping!' whispered
a young constable to his right.

'That's the buckle of his belt knocking against the edge
of the table,' pointed out an older officer, facing him.

'The table moved!' insisted the constable. 'I felt it move!'

'Lord help us, you're right! The blooming thing's coming
alive!'

The medium had grown noticeably more pink. His eyes
remained closed and his hands stayed firmly on the table,
which was unquestionably mobile. The vibrations seemed
to originate at the opposite end, where a stoutly-built
sergeant was seated. The table looked like shortly achieving
sufficient momentum to overturn altogether, but a timely

3

stiffening of the medium's arms restored stability. At the same time he emerged sufficiently from his trance to glare across the table.

'Spirits are agitated tonight,' said the fat sergeant, in justification.

'Perhaps they've got a message for us,' suggested the young constable.

'Wait a bit,' said the medium in a strange voice. 'There's something coming through.'

The officers round the table peered expectantly at him as he began to moan. At the far end of the room a large, bearded detective-constable continued unconcernedly with the report he was writing.

'Is there someone there?' asked the medium, addressing his remark to the ceiling.

The flame in the gas-lamp above the table might have leapt a quarter-inch higher, but there was no other appreciable response.

'Are you trying to get through?'

Three faint knocks were heard from under the table.

'Did you hear that?' demanded the young constable.

'That's one of 'em for sure,' confirmed the sergeant, shuffling in his chair. 'It's their way of communicating. Three knocks for yes, one for no.'

'Do you have a message for one of us?' the medium asked the spirit.

The three knocks were repeated, more boldly.

'Is it for the sergeant, here?'

One knock indicated that it was not.

'The constable on my left?'

One knock.

'The one on my right, then?'

4

The young constable sighed in relief as the spirit excluded him, too.

The medium frowned. 'Is it for me, then?'

One knock.

'Well, who the hell *is* it for?' the fat sergeant demanded.

This time the spirit disdained to reply.

'Can't make up its blooming mind.'

'Stop your jaw a moment,' said the medium. 'I'll tell you what we're going to do. *You* can ask the questions, and we'll invite the spirit to use my voice to answer 'em. That's how all the regular mediums work. Give me a moment first to clear my mind of worldly thoughts.' He closed his eyes again, and presently slumped forward on the table with his head between his hands.

With a glance at his companions, the fat sergeant put the first question: 'Are you still there?'

'Yes,' intoned the voice of the medium, a shade thicker than before.

'Do you have a message?'

'Yes.'

'Who is it for?'

'One what is present, but not at the table.'

The fat sergeant turned in his chair to look at the only other occupant of the room, still diligently writing his report. 'Well, of all the . . . It's for you, Thackeray!'

Detective-Constable Edward Thackeray wiped the nib of his pen and put it down. 'Eh? What did you say?'

'The message. It's for you.'

'What message?'

'From the spirit.'

'Oh,' said Thackeray, without much interest. 'I don't hold much with that sort of caper.'

5

'Wait. We'll see who it comes from.' He addressed the spirit in a solemn voice. 'Who are you?'

'Charlie,' said the medium.

'I don't know anyone called Charlie,' said Thackeray, and picked up his pen, as if that settled the matter.

'Charlie Peace,' boomed the spirit voice, unsolicited.

Thackeray wheeled round. Everyone at Paradise Street knew that he owed his place in the Criminal Investigation Department to the part he had played in arresting the notorious Peace in 1878. It was his principal topic of mess-room conversation.

'Would that be Charlie Peace, the Banner Cross murderer?' queried the fat sergeant, with a wink at his companions.

'The same,' said the voice.

'I don't believe it,' said Thackeray, in a tone suggesting the opposite.

'Swung for me crimes at Leeds Prison seven years back,' added the spirit voice, by way of amplification. 'And might 'ave been walkin' the earth today, robbin' and murderin' me fellow-creatures, if it wasn't for Constable Thackeray.'

'That's a fact, at any rate,' said Thackeray. 'Haven't I always told you blokes as much?'

'Why, so you have,' said the fat sergeant. 'As much, and a sight more sometimes, wouldn't you say, mates?'

There were nods and winks all round.

'Let's find out what the message is, then,' he continued. 'If Charlie Peace has come voluntary into a police station it *must* be important.' He looked at the ceiling. 'What do you want to say to Constable Thackeray, Charlie?'

The bowed figure of the medium did not move. 'I 'ave come with a summons for Constable Thackeray.'

'A summons?' repeated Thackeray.

'Well, that's a change,' said the sergeant. 'Charlie serving a summons on one of *us*.'

'Are you there, Thackeray?' asked the voice.

Thackeray got to his feet like a schoolboy named in class. 'Why, yes. I suppose I am.'

'Then you must prepare yourself. I 'ave come to tell you that you are shortly goin' on a journey.'

'A journey? Where to?'

There was a pause. 'To the Other Side.'

Thackeray's jaw dropped open. 'The Other Side?'

Quite without warning the medium discharged himself from his trance and sat upright, a broad grin across his face. 'Yes, Thackeray, the Other Side. Of the river, of course. Message from Great Scotland Yard came in by despatch-cart this evening. You're commanded to report to Sergeant Cribb at nine o'clock sharp tomorrow morning.'

With satisfying slowness, the realization that he had been hoaxed dawned on Thackeray's face. The others were laughing too much to escape the bombardment of bound volumes of the *Police Gazette* that presently hurtled across the room.

Although it was several months since they had worked together, Sergeant Cribb wasted no time on cordialities when Thackeray reported next morning.

'Keep your coat on, Constable. We're not staying here.'

No offer of a mug of Scotland Yard cocoa to revive a man's circulation on a frosty November morning. Lord no, that wasn't Cribb's style at all. Instead, a rapid inspection with the gimlet eyes.

'You look older, Thackeray.'

'That must be the frost on my beard, Sarge. I couldn't get a place inside the bus. Had to travel on top.'

'You'd keep in better shape if you walked.'

Thackeray grimaced at the thought. 'Have a heart! It's over three miles from Rotherhithe, Sarge.'

'You'd do it under the hour, easy. I don't like to see a man go soft just because he's taken off the beat to do detective work. Now trot downstairs and stop a cab, will you? We're off to Burlington House.'

'The Royal Academy? We can walk that in twenty minutes,' Thackeray volunteered. 'It's under a mile. I ain't *that* decrepit.'

Cribb shook his head. 'Not this time, Thackeray. It's not the class of place you approach on foot. When you go to the Royal Academy you drive through the arch and round the courtyard to the entrance. It's a first principle of plain clothes work that you don't draw attention to yourself by behaving erratic.'

Thackeray had guessed there would be *some* good reason for taking a cab. There inevitably was when Cribb was planning a journey.

By half past nine they were being escorted up the main staircase of Burlington House by the keeper. The galleries were not opened to the public before eleven, but he recognized and admitted the 'detective gentlemen' at once, for all Cribb's care over the first principle of plain clothes work.

On the top floor they entered a long room hung with large canvases in ornate gilt frames.

'The new Diploma Gallery,' announced the keeper.

At the far end, a familiar figure in a silk hat was studying a picture.

8

'Looks as if Inspector Jowett has become a patron of the arts,' Cribb remarked to Thackeray. 'Thank you, Keeper. We'll join the other gentleman now.'

They got within a few yards of the inspector before he side-stepped slickly away from the subject of his study, a larger-than-life rendering of the Judgment of Paris, and faced them from the less distracting backcloth of a still life with pheasants. 'Ah, Sergeant Cribb,' he said, putting away a pair of *pince-nez* neither detective had ever seen him use before. 'Your first visit to the Academy, I dare say.'

'Quite correct, sir. The only portraits I get to see are the ones in the Convict Office.'

'So I expected. In this suite of galleries you will find the work of the Academicians themselves. Each one, when he is elected, has to deposit a painting or sculpture known as his diploma work. To your left, Sergeant, is a Gainsborough.'

'You don't say so, sir!' said Cribb, with some attempt at awe.

'And within a few feet of us are a Reynolds and a Turner.'

'And a Constable sir,' Thackeray innocently added.

The back of Inspector Jowett's neck stiffened. The air was thick with possibilities of insubordination.

'And there's a Landseer,' said Cribb quickly.

'I think we had better address ourselves to the reason for our presence here,' said Jowett, after an interval. 'I want you most particularly to examine the Etty over here.'

He led them to a canvas largely occupied by the reclining form of a young woman, naked save for a wisp of fabric draped artfully over the hip. Her arms were curled above her head in the abandon of sleep. A creature half-human, half-goat, was in the act of lifting a sheet that had seemingly provided an adequate covering a moment before. A second creature of the same genus was trying to restrain his companion. It was entitled *Sleeping Nymph and Satyrs.*

'Do you have any observations?' Jowett asked, facing the painting.

Cribb, unschooled in criticism of the Fine Arts, said nothing.

Thackeray filled the breach. 'The one with the sheet looks a bit like Percy Alleway of C Division.'

Out of sight of Jowett, Cribb jerked his hand in a desperate gesture of constraint. To his surprise the inspector turned on Thackeray with an expansive smile. 'Splendid, Constable! It is manifestly clear from what you say that you are examining the painting as a good detective should, attempting to find some detail that will fix it indelibly in your memory. That is exactly what I have brought you here to do. Continue, if you please. You, too, Sergeant.' He gripped Cribb's arm and brought him closer to the nymph, as if introducing a bloodhound to the scent. 'Neglect nothing. The disposition of the limbs. The highlighting of the flesh. There's nothing in the Royal Academy unfit for Scotland Yard to set its eyes upon, you know.' Then he stepped away along the gallery, leaving the two of them in uncomfortable surveillance of the picture. After a suitable interval he returned. 'All committed to memory? I knew I could rely on you both. It is most important, you see, that you recognize this scene when you see it again, as I trust you will before long.'

Cribb frowned at the canvas, pondering over Jowett's

meaning. Was this visit to the Academy going to become a regular thing, then – some ill-conceived attempt by the Home Office to bring sweetness and light into the lives of the lower ranks? 'You want us to recognize it again, sir?'

'That was the burden of my remarks, Sergeant. I hope I made myself clear.'

'You did, sir.' Cribb paused, and asked, 'You weren't expecting someone to try and steal it?'

'Oh no. The stealing has been done. I want you to recover it.'

Cribb shook his head. 'You've lost me now, sir.'

'Really? Perhaps one ought to explain that Etty painted two versions of his *Sleeping Nymph*, identical except in certain trivial details. The first was in effect a practice piece for this, his diploma work. It is the first version that has been stolen. It was the property until last week of an acquaintance of mine not entirely unknown in the world of science.'

'Science?' repeated Cribb, eyeing the canvas again.

'A man of cultivated taste,' Jowett went on. 'A member of the Royal Society. I don't suppose you will have heard of him. Dr Probert.'

'Dr Probert's Pick-me-up?' interjected Thackeray. 'I'm never without a bottle, sir.'

'Not *that* Dr Probert,' said Jowett icily. 'Dr Probert of the University of London, the eminent physiologist. A man of the most refined taste. I was with him socially only yesterday evening. He is most exercised over the loss of his Etty. He has asked me personally to ensure its recovery.'

'So you brought us here to see one?' said Cribb.

'Just so.' Jowett appeared relieved that he was making

11

himself clear again. 'It is fortunate that we have this version for you to examine.'

'But you mentioned some differences from the original.'

'Yes. Quite unimportant. Dr Probert's painting is without the piece of material here that is draped over the – er – hip. Doubtless Etty was mindful that his diploma work would go on public exhibition. Ladies, you know. The first version has always been privately owned. Few people know of its existence, which makes the theft all the more difficult to account for.'

'Was anything else taken?'

'Nothing at all. Strange, that. Dr Probert has a number of other paintings in his house at Richmond, all of classical subjects. Alma Tadema, Leighton, that sort of thing—'

'Mostly young women like this one in a state of nature?' Cribb suggested.

'That's neither here nor there, Sergeant. Dr Probert went to Charterhouse. He had a schooling in the classics.'

'And the Etty was the only picture that went,' said Cribb, returning crisply to the matter under investigation. 'Do we have any other information to go on, sir?'

'Only a rather strange coincidence. The picture was stolen last Friday evening, when Dr Probert was giving a lantern lecture at University College Hospital. His wife and daughter were in the audience and only one of his servants was at home, an old woman, prone to deafness. She noticed nothing irregular, but when the Proberts returned, the Etty was gone. The curious thing is that the previous Saturday the Proberts had given a dinner party for a number of their friends, and on the same night one of them, a Miss Crush, returned to find that *her* house had been burgled.'

12

'Could be interesting,' said Cribb. 'What was stolen?'

'Ah,' Jowett wagged a cautionary finger at Cribb. 'You think I'm going to say that it was a picture. It was not, Sergeant. It was a Royal Worcester vase in the Japanese style.'

'Valuable, sir?'

'Not outstandingly. It was worth perhaps thirty pounds. On the same sideboard from which it was taken was a Minton vase by Solon valued at more than a thousand guineas.'

Cribb whistled. 'What sort of a cracksman misses a chance like that?' Shaking his head at such criminal negligence, he asked, 'What did he fill his sack with, for Heaven's sake?'

'Interestingly enough,' said Jowett, 'the housebreaker contented himself with a single object – as did the picture-thief at Dr Probert's, you will have observed.'

Thackeray nodded his head to show that he, at any rate, had not missed the point.

'This Miss Crush, sir,' said Cribb. 'She's obviously a rich woman. Would you describe her as a close friend of Dr Probert's?'

Jowett gave a small sigh. 'Sergeant, you must not permit your animosity to anyone of a superior social status to yourself to vitiate your deductive processes. No, Miss Crush is not a close friend of Dr Probert's. She is merely an acquaintance. They met three weeks ago at a small gathering at her house in Belgravia. The doctor was invited in his capacity as an eminent man of science.'

'For his conversation?'

'No, Sergeant. He was there to bring the scientific mind to bear on a phenomenon that is rarely, if ever, examined by the analytical methods of the laboratory. Miss Crush's "At Home", and the dinner party that was subsequently held at the Proberts' house, were both arranged for a similar purpose. A spiritualistic seance.'

'Well, I'll be jiggered!' said Thackeray.

2

Who finds a picture, digs a medal up,
Hits on a first edition – he henceforth
Gives it his name, grows notable: how much more,
Who ferrets out a 'medium'?

There was the start of a smile on Cribb's face as he marched up the steep incline of Richmond Hill towards Dr Probert's residence. It was a long time since he had investigated a burglary. Out in the Divisions they didn't like seeking the assistance of the Yard for anything less than murder. What had happened here was exceptional, of course. A personal approach to Jowett from Dr Probert. Jowett with his notions of hobnobbing with the upper crust wasn't going to turn down an appeal like that. Not from a member of the Royal Society. The Richmond police had scarcely got the case into the Occurrence Book before it was taken over by the C.I.D.

Cribb understood the reason. There was a reputation to protect. Local bobbies talked too freely to the Press. Probert didn't want to pick up his *Richmond and Twickenham Times* and read about the gallery of naked nymphs and goddesses and the communications with the spirits at the house on Richmond Hill.

But it was not the peculiarities of the present case that brought the smile to Cribb's lips. It was his relish for a burglary. Unlike murder or assault, housebreaking was a bit of a game, and self-respecting cracksmen played it with sufficient skill to test the best detectives. The prize was property. Occasionally the game was spoiled by unnecessary violence, but generally it was splendid entertainment. As good as an evening at the Poker table.

Probert's house, tall, detached and Georgian, was near the top of the Hill, almost opposite the Terrace. Below, a persistent river-mist obscured the Thames Valley, but at this level you could see for miles above the mist. It produced a disturbing impression of isolation.

Before pulling at the doorbell, Cribb cast an eye over the ground-floor windows. They were all equipped with substantial shutters. The thief hadn't entered that way if the servants had done their work. It would have made more sense, anyway, to break in from the back, where there was no chance of attracting the attention of promenaders on the Terrace.

Like any police officer worthy of the name, Cribb had a confident way with servants, but the one who opened the door looked difficult from the start. She was far too long in the tooth for a parlour-maid, and she knew it. He judged it wise to try the straightforward approach, politely introducing himself and stating his business. He might have saved his breath. She told him in a firm, toneless voice that Dr Probert didn't buy things at the front door and they didn't want him trying the trades-men's entrance either. Plainly she was deaf. He remembered Jowett mentioning a servant who had heard nothing on the night of the burglary. He tried a second time, with gestures, but made no more impression. Then, feeling in his pocket for a pencil and notebook, he brought out the handcuffs he habitually carried. They worked as well as a visiting-card.

He was shown through an ill-lit hall into a drawing-room where a fire blazed, its flames reproduced in miniature on multitudinous 'brights' – brass, copper and silver ornaments and embellishments. He crossed to the fireplace, an immense black marble structure with an overmantel of gilded wood that reached to the ceiling, and spread his palms to warm them, assuming (quite erroneously, as it turned out) that Dr Probert reckoned detective-sergeants suitable persons to shake by the hand.

It was his practice on entering a strange room to make a rapid mental inventory of its contents and their positions. One like this, so closely lined with furniture that not an inch of skirting-board was visible, and with every ledge and shelf covered with a silk runner and crowded with objects, presented a severe test. He decided to take it by sections, starting with all he could see reflected in the mirror over the mantelpiece. Principally, this was a tall black lacquered cabinet with mother-of-pearl inlay. He was surveying its contents in the mirror when he noticed with surprise that the object beside the cabinet, quite eclipsed by an adjacent potted palm, was no object at all, but a woman, sitting perfectly still.

'I must apologize, ma'am,' he said, turning. 'I quite failed to notice you as I came in.'

'People frequently do,' she said. 'There is no need to apologize. My husband has failed to notice me for years now. I am quite resigned to it. You must be the inspector from the police.'

17

'Sergeant only, ma'am,' he admitted. 'Cribb is my name.'

'And mine is Probert – although it might as well be anything else,' she said, easing her wedding-ring absently along the length of her finger. 'I am quite unsuited to play the part of Dr Probert's wife.'

Cribb frowned and rubbed his side-whiskers. This was not a form of drawing-room conversation he had met before. Clearly he was obliged to say something to bolster Mrs Probert's self-respect. But what? Looking at her under the palm fronds, pale, slight and even-featured, with the far-away expression artists gave the models in corsetry advertisements, he could understand perfectly how her husband failed to notice her. 'That's a handsome plant you're sitting under, ma'am,' he said.

'Thank you. I like to sit here away from the fire. I don't have any faith in complexion-shields. There's one in the hearth there that I embroidered myself, but I have never risked using it. They are not an adequate protection for a delicate skin, Sergeant. Just as dangerous as parasols.'

'I'm sure,' said Cribb. 'You'll pardon me for mentioning it, but I wondered whether I made the purpose of my visit quite clear to your servant. She seems slightly . . .' He patted his right ear.

'Yes, we have noticed it,' said Mrs Probert. 'She has been with us for nearly twenty years, though. You may be quite sure that she has told my husband you are here. If I bore you, please don't hesitate to tell me.'

'No fear of that, ma'am,' said Cribb emphatically. 'Do you have any other servants?'

'Two house-maids and a cook, naturally. They were all out on the night the picture was stolen, except Hitchman,

18

whom you have met. We try to give them an evening off once a month and it suited us to arrange it that night, when we attended my husband's lecture at the Hospital. Hitchman didn't hear a thing, of course. My husband was most awfully discomposed by what we found when we returned, and said some unrepeatable things. I was more than a little grateful Hitchman could not hear them.'

'And you informed the police next morning, I understand.'

'Yes, it was much too late to do anything about it that night, so we went to bed.'

'A pity, that,' said Cribb. 'There's always an officer on the beat in the locality. You could have sent a servant to find him. The thief might well have been hiding somewhere in your garden.'

'Really? What a gruesome thought!'

'He'd be unlikely to take to the streets with a stolen picture before midnight. I dare say there's people moving about until the small hours up here on the Hill.'

'Yes, one hears footsteps and voices. Even carriages. I cannot think what attracts people to the Terrace so late at night.'

It was no part of Cribb's duty to enlighten her, so he turned to another matter. 'I believe the entry was made through a window in the basement, ma'am.'

'That is so. I am sure my husband will wish to show you. It was a most audacious crime. Do you know, he got in through a barred window?'

'I expected it, ma'am,' said Cribb. 'That's the easiest means of entry, short of using a latch-key. All you need is a length of rope and a strong metal rod. You pass a double loop round two bars, insert the rod between the strands and twist it round to draw the bars together. I see that you have shutters at the front of your house. Pity you don't have them at the back as well. Bars are a false economy, in my opinion.'

'Your opinion was not asked for, Policeman. You are here to solve a crime, not to redesign my house.' The speaker, just inside the door, must have been standing there for several seconds. 'In case your deductive powers are not equal to the task, I should tell you that my name is Probert.'

'And this is Sergeant Cribb, Augustus, from Scotland Yard,' said his wife.

Ignoring her, Probert flung open the door and left the room.

'You had better go with him,' Mrs Probert advised. 'He intends to show you his picture-gallery.'

'I see. Will you be coming too, ma'am?'

She shook her head firmly. 'That is not permitted. Doubtless I shall see you later, Sergeant. Please hurry. He is not a patient man.'

'In here, Policeman,' boomed Probert from across the hall. Cribb entered a narrow room carpeted in crimson and furnished with sideboard, black chaise longue and in the centre a fine example of the curiosity known as a flirtation settee, shaped like the letter S, with seats in the curves, so that sitters would face opposite ways, yet be side by side. Probert already occupied one section and was impatiently beating the other with his right hand.

'Sit yourself down, man. I'm not too proud to share a seat with a public servant, but I'm damned if I want him staring me in the face.'

The sentiment was mutual, but Cribb refrained from saying so. What little he had seen of Probert, the squat physique topped by a disproportionately large bald head, the bulbous blue eyes and the sandy-haired moustache waxed at the ends, he did not like. The single thing in favour of the man was that his house had been burgled. For this, Cribb took his place on the flirtation settee.

'I don't propose to beat about the bush,' said Dr Probert. 'My wife misunderstands me.'

'Really?' said Cribb, uncertain what was required of him.

'My own fault absolutely. Married her for her father's money. She's given me all of that, a handsome daughter and twenty-one years of boredom. So what have I done to keep my sanity? I've found distractions. Look at the wall ahead of you.'

It was a superfluous instruction.

'What do you see?'

'Curtains,' said Cribb. 'Black velvet curtains. At least a dozen sets of them.'

'Get up and pull the draw-string at the side of any one of them.'

Cribb went to the largest, gripped the tassel and watched as the curtains parted at the centre and drew smoothly away to reveal the painting of a woman reclining face downwards among cushions on a sofa. She was naked.

'What is the title on the frame?' asked Dr Probert, from his side of the S.

'*Reclining Nymph,*' answered Cribb.

'Ah yes, the Boucher. I went to Paris to buy that. A portrait by the artist of his own wife in a classical pose.

21

She is exquisite. Draw the curtain again, please. One cannot be too discreet when there are ladies in the house. My wife and daughter clearly understand that they must not set foot inside this room, but you never know what's going on where women are concerned. They are a perverse sex, I tell you, Policeman. They are quite capable of convincing themselves that something is going on in here that compels them to ignore my instructions. The most fanciful inventions – a fire, for example.'

'Or a burglary?' suggested Cribb, and quickly added, 'Some of these pictures must be very valuable, sir.'

'Indeed, yes, but they are all insured. Would you like to see some more? I have a magnificent *Rape of the Sabine Women* on this wall.'

'Thank you, sir, but not just now. We policemen come across quite enough of that sort of thing in our work. I should like to see where the stolen picture was hanging, if you don't mind.'

'The Etty?' Dr Probert stood up and went to one of the larger sets of curtains on the wall in front of him and pulled the cord. An empty frame was revealed. 'The scoundrel removed the canvas from the frame. I hope to Heaven that the surface wasn't damaged. Oh, Policeman, the tone of that young woman's skin! Pure alabaster. You'll get it back, of course?'

'I'm going to try,' said Cribb. 'Tell me, sir, was it your most valuable picture?'

'My word, no! The value is sentimental. A mere three hundred guineas, if my insurers know anything about art. I have an Ingres worth ten times that.'

Cribb lifted the frame away from the wall and looked behind it. 'He worked quickly. Look at the way these metal supports have been forced. He risked tearing the edge of the canvas as he prised it away from the frame. This is rough work for a picture-thief. As a rule they take more care. If a dealer sees that a canvas has been forced from a frame he has to be told a very convincing story before he'll make an offer for it. This was the only picture that was touched – is that right, sir?'

'That is my firm opinion,' said Dr Probert, 'and Inspector Jowett confirms it. I invited him here to make his own examination of every picture after I had refused the same facility to two constables from Richmond police station. I don't show my collection to every Tom, Dick and Harry, blast 'em! I showed them the window that was forced, of course. I'll show that to any damned fool. If you've finished in here I'll take you down to see it straight away.'

After several years' service with Jowett, Cribb was practically impervious to insults, particularly when they had the reassuring ring of spontaneity. He followed Probert into the passage and down the basement stairs. 'I'll have to light a candle,' said Probert in a carrying voice. 'We don't have the new electric light down here.' On cue, a maid appeared ahead, candle in hand. 'That will do, Pearce,' said Probert, taking it. 'You can get back to your work now. Too damned inquisitive,' he told Cribb. 'You'd think they'd never clapped eyes on a common policeman before.' He opened the door of a pantry stacked high with jars, tins and boxes. 'There it is above the biscuits. Now tell me I should have had shutters instead of bars, like all the rest.'

'Can I have the candle over here, sir?' asked Cribb, moving to the window. 'I see you've had some repairs done.'

He indicated the shining heads of fresh nails that had been used to hammer the close-meshed wire netting back into place.

'Naturally! I wasn't having the ruffian come back for all my other pictures,' said Dr Probert. 'If he isn't a professional picture-thief as you seem to suggest, what on earth did he do it for? Was it anything to do with the subject of the picture, do you suppose? I believe there are men about who look at pictures like mine for the wrong reasons, if you follow me.'

'Indeed,' said Cribb solemnly, and added, without changing his expression, 'Equally, it could be a man with a special interest in the classics, such as yourself. Whoever it is obviously knows a lot about the workings of your household.'

'Do you think so?'

'I'm certain of it. He chose the one evening when you and your family were out of the house, and the only servant at home was Hitchman, who is deaf. He knew where to break in and how to locate the gallery. Do many of your friends visit the house, sir?'

'Precious few. I am far too occupied with my work to have a social life. Aren't you going to measure the window, or something? All the others did.'

'In that case, there's no need for me to do the same,' said Cribb. 'My assistant, Constable Thackeray, is at Richmond police station at this moment going through the reports of the officers who first investigated the crime. I dare say they checked outside for footprints.'

'Indeed they did,' said Probert, 'but they didn't find any. It's a tiled court out there. If you've finished, shall we go upstairs? I find it devilish draughty down here.'

'You say you have no social life,' said Cribb, as if he had not heard, 'but Inspector Jowett mentioned a spot of table-turning that took place here.'

Probert cleared his throat awkwardly. 'The seance? Yes, I had some people here the Saturday before last, but it was more in the nature of an experiment – an extension of my work, in fact – than a social occasion.'

'Really, sir? I thought communicating with the spirits was all the rage at the moment. No party is complete without a medium, or so the gossip goes.'

'Oh no,' said Probert. 'This wasn't party games. It was a scientific experiment, the first of a series I have under-taken to conduct with the medium concerned. The next one is taking place on Saturday. We are merely searchers after the truth.'

'I see. Who are these searchers, sir?'

'Oh, I can vouch for every one of them.'

'I should like to know their names, even so,' said Cribb.

'No, no, these were my guests. Respectable people, every one. I'm not having them subjected to an inquisition simply because they visited my house in the interests of science a few days before it was burgled. Blast it, I'd rather forget the whole damned thing!'

Cribb was not so lightly brushed aside. 'One was Miss Crush, whose house you visited for a similar purpose on – ' he took out his notebook '– the 15th October. I shall be seeing Miss Crush this afternoon, sir. I expect she'll give me the names, but I do dislike having to press a lady for information. It's even more distasteful to me than bribing the domestics. But there you are – it's my living.'

'Bribing the domestics?' repeated Dr Probert, aghast.

25

'We only do it if the information ain't forthcoming as it should be. No, I'll put the screws on Miss Crush before I resort to that.'

'Good Lord!' said Probert. 'Jowett promised to send somebody discreet. Look here, I'm not having that good lady victimized.'

'Better tell me who was at the seance, then, sir,' said Cribb in his most reasonable manner.

'Very well, Policeman, but don't push me too far. There were five people round the table that evening in addition to myself: Miss Crush; my daughter Alice and her fiancé, William Nye; Henry Strathmore, a fellow scientist; and Brand, the medium.'

'Wasn't there someone else, sir?'

Dr Probert frowned. 'I'm damned sure there wasn't. Oh, I see!' He gave a sheepish smile. 'You mean the spirit visitor?'

'No sir,' said Cribb. 'I was thinking of your wife.'

'Winifred? She wasn't there. She refuses to have anything to do with our experiments. She's terrified of the supernatural. Won't even walk through the churchyard to the Parish Church on a Sunday morning unless I take her firmly by the arm. She spent the evening of the seance locked in the bathroom reading back numbers of *The Tatler*. She said it was the place where a ghost was least likely to manifest itself.'

'But your daughter must be made of sterner stuff.'

'Ah, yes. You won't have met Alice.' Dr Probert's face lit with pride. 'There's no question of it. She takes after me. She has the inquiring mind of the Probert side. No nonsense about Alice, I can tell you. She'd make a first-rate scientist, given the opportunity.'

26

'I take it that she has some other occupation then, sir?'

'Good God, no. She isn't in *employment*, if that's what you mean. She's very active in the parish. Charitable work: distributing the produce of the Harvest Festival to the poor, and so forth. My word, yes. To see young Alice striding down the Hill with a marrow under her arm in search of a destitute family is a stirring sight, I promise you.'

'I wouldn't have thought there were many families of that sort hereabouts,' said Cribb.

'Quite so. She has the devil of a job locating them in Richmond. But she's inexhaustible. And what she can't dispose of we put to good use here. Nothing is wasted, I assure you. Look here, if you've finished looking at the window we'll go upstairs to the civilized level of the house.'

They returned to the drawing-room where Mrs Probert was still seated. True to her account of things, Dr Probert ignored her presence altogether. 'D'you smoke, Policeman? No? Then you won't mind if I light a cigar, I dare say. Yes, I'm sorry you haven't met Alice, but she's already out on some charitable excursion.'

'Buying a hat in the High Street,' said Mrs Probert.

'Her fiancé William is a public-spirited young fellow, too,' continued Probert, as if nothing had been said. 'Bought himself a commission in the East Surreys. That boy would be an asset to any regiment. Carries himself immaculately. I'm always reminded of a camel when I look at him – the supreme dignity of its bearing, you understand, nothing else.'

'I shall make a point of looking for it when I meet him,

sir,' said Cribb. 'You mentioned another guest – Mr Strathmore, was it?'

'Yes. A highly respected figure in the field of psychical investigation. He is one of the Lads.'

'The fast set, sir?'

'No, the Life After Death Society. The members are all men of science interested in investigating the occult. I believe Strathmore is the secretary. He also happens to be the leading craniologist in London. I know him professionally, you see.'

'Had he been to your house before last week, sir?'

'No, there was no occasion for it. We took drinks together in our clubs and discovered a mutual interest in spiritualistic phenomena. When I decided to hold a seance at my house, I invited Strathmore. It was the obvious thing to do. He's not the sort to help himself to another chap's pictures, if that's the way your suspicious mind is drifting. He's a gentleman, damn it.'

So were several others Cribb could name languishing in Newgate, Wormwood Scrubs and Coldbath Fields, but he declined to mention them. He would form his own assessment of Strathmore later. 'And was the seance worthy of Mr Strathmore's visit, sir?'

'Eminently worthy. We had the most impressive seance of phenomena – table-rapping, voices, messages pertaining to be from the Other Side. I preserve an open mind, of course, and so does Strathmore, but one cannot deny that certain things happened that night which are devilish difficult to explain.'

'*Devilish* is the proper word for it,' commented Mrs Probert, looking into the fire.

She seemed to expect no return for her utterances, so

Cribb went on: 'I've one other question about that night, sir. It doesn't concern the table-rapping or the voices. It might be just as significant to my inquiry, though. Did you by any chance mention to the guests your forthcoming lecture at University College Hospital?'

'Certainly I did,' said Probert. 'It's the sort of thing that comes up naturally in conversation.'

'Of course, sir. Let's return to Mr Brand. I believe he's making quite a reputation as a medium. He's much in demand, from what I understand.'

'The whole of London will soon be clamouring to see him,' said Probert. 'And no wonder. He is the most promising member of his profession since D. D. Home. I had the greatest difficulty engaging him for my series of experiments. We have only got him next Saturday thanks to an outbreak of scarlet fever at Lady Millmont's. He restricts his engagements to two a week because of the strain on his vital powers.'

'Yet he is quite young, I understand,' said Cribb.

'Twenty-two, but communicating with the spirits takes a dreadful toll on a man, whatever his age. And Brand is not robust. He is quite humble in origin, the son of a Blackheath cabman, I am told, and he has the under-nourished look of the less fortunate class. It would not surprise me if he died young.'

'Nor me,' added Mrs Probert. 'It would be a judgment.'

'Where did you first meet him?' Cribb inquired.

'At Miss Crush's house in Eaton Square,' said Probert.

'Ah, yes. The first seance. And was that just as successful as yours, sir?'

'I'm bound to admit that it was. Some of those round the table even spoke of witnessing a materialization, a spirit

29

hand hovering in the air, but I missed it myself. All the audible phenomena were present. It was because they so impressed me that I invited Brand to my own house for a programme of seances on scientific principles. Naturally I invited Miss Crush, my hostess, as well.'

'Did you invite any other members of her party?'

'Brand, of course. Nobody else. The others at Kensington were neighbours of Miss Crush, the Bratts.'

'I beg your pardon, sir.'

'The Bratts, I said. Sir Hartley Bratt and his wife and daughter. Sir Hartley is ninety years of age and wouldn't want to drive as far as Richmond even if I asked him. He has a suspect heart.'

'At ninety, that's not surprising,' said Cribb. 'I shouldn't think communing with the spirits would be good for him either.'

'On the contrary. He is a confirmed spiritualist. Most of his friends have passed over and keeping in touch gives him an interest in life. Well, Policeman, we seem to have ventured a long way from my stolen Etty, unless you are proposing to arrest Sir Hartley Bratt. What conclusions have you reached?'

'Only one of any note, sir. For the present I'm assuming a connection between the thefts of your Etty and Miss Crush's Royal Worcester vase. Each took place a matter of days after a seance at the house in question. Now lifting a picture ain't quite the same thing as lifting a vase, I'll admit, but it might be of significance that the thief in each case had the chance of taking something more valuable, and missed it.'

'That's very pertinent, now you mention it,' said Dr Probert.

'If it *is* significant, sir, the list of guests at those two seances is crucial to my inquiry. From what you tell me there was one person, and one only, who attended both seances, apart from Miss Crush and yourself.'

'Brand,' said Mrs Probert from her place under the palm. 'Peter Brand, the medium.'

3

Pray do you find guests criticize your wine,
Your furniture, your grammar, or your nose?
Then, why your 'medium'? What's the difference?

Miss Crush was more observant of rank than Dr Probert. '*Sergeant,*' she said, as Cribb was announced by the maid. 'Such excitement! Do come in, Sergeant, and let me look at you.'

He took two short steps into the room – short not from shyness, but because a rosewood table, circular in shape, barred his way. At the centre was a tall Copeland vase containing pink chrysanthemums a little past their prime. From where he stood, Miss Crush's face regarded him through a space between the blooms. It was delicate, compact and fringed with fair, slightly dishevelled hair.

'You have the look of a sensitive,' said Miss Crush.

'A detective actually, ma'am,' Cribb gently explained.

'Yes, but there is definitely something about you, I felt it as soon as the door opened and I feel it more strongly now. You *must* be a sensitive. It doesn't prevent you from being a detective as well, you know. I should think it would be a positive advantage. What did my maid say your surname was?'

'Cribb, ma'am.'

'Superb! Sensitive Sergeant Cribb – how do you like that?'

'If I'm honest, ma'am, I prefer my official rank. I'm here about your vase.'

'Never mind that,' said Miss Crush. 'Do you ever notice atmospheres – when you first enter a room, for instance?'

It seemed she was not referring to the faintly stale scent of the chrysanthemums.

'Or do you feel invisible presences?' Miss Crush continued.

Cribb shook his head. 'I'm strictly interested in facts, ma'am. Feelings don't enter into it much in my job. The vase was taken last Friday evening, I believe.'

'Yes, but it's of no consequence now. It was not one of my better pieces. I gave a description to the young constable who called on Saturday. He was perfectly civil, but he was not a sensitive. Do you ever have visionary experiences?'

'Not in the course of duty, ma'am. Was the vase taken from this room?'

Miss Crush got to her feet and came round the table to place a hand on Cribb's sleeve. She was small and fortyish. She either used rouge, or the excitement of discovering a sensitive had gone to her cheeks. 'If you *will* persist with your questions I shall try to answer them, but I really do not mind about the vase. It was taken a week ago last Saturday from the sideboard over there while I was at Dr Probert's for a seance. The thief got in through the mews at the back of the house and opened a door by removing one of the panes, putting his arm through and unfastening

33

the latch. The servants were in the kitchen and didn't hear a thing – playing cards, I shouldn't wonder. I got home shortly after midnight and heard about the broken pane when Annie, my parlour-maid, was locking up half an hour later. It wasn't until morning that we found the vase had gone.'

'Didn't you check to see if anything was stolen after you found the window broken?' asked Cribb, incredulously.

'You know how it is, Sergeant. One is always wiser after the event. I was already in bed when Annie came to tell me what she had found, and I must confess that I was in a state of some perturbation about the manifestations the medium had produced at Dr Probert's. To be frank, I was disinclined to venture downstairs by candlelight. I directed Annie to look into each of the rooms, thinking that if a burglar had visited us the fact would be only too apparent. I never suspected he would be content with a single vase, and a common piece of Worcester at that.'

'It was still worth thirty pounds, I understand, ma'am. That's as much as your Annie would earn in a year, I dare say.'

'Quite true, but I'm sure she didn't take it. I allowed the constable to search her box, just in case. Besides, why should she want to break a window?'

'I wasn't venturing to accuse your servant, ma'am,' Cribb primly said. 'I was simply trying to make the point that thirty pounds is a tidy sum by ordinary people's standards. You had quite a lively seance at Dr Probert's then, if lively is the word to use in the circumstances.'

Miss Crush started to giggle and stifled it with a lace handkerchief. 'My word, yes. The dear departed were coming through very clearly. Mr Brand is set to become the most successful medium in London. The evening began with table-tapping, which is quite usual, but by the end of the evening the spirits were speaking through his voice, a man and a woman coming through very distinctly.'

'Remarkable,' said Cribb.

'Indeed, yes. They conveyed a message to me.'

'Nothing to do with your house being burgled?'

Miss Crush frowned. 'No. They are not concerned with worldly matters once they have gone over to the Other Side. It was to tell me that my late Uncle Walter is well content where he is. He made an unfortunate marriage, poor man, and my aunt frequently drove him to distraction. There was no mention of her in the message, although she followed him only two months after his going.'

'It's an extensive place, I understand,' said Cribb. 'If your uncle kept moving . . .'

'Quite so.'

Cribb skirted the table to examine the sideboard where the stolen vase had stood. At least a dozen others were on parade there in two ranks.

'It isn't missed,' said Miss Crush, following him. 'I simply changed the positions of the others and now you wouldn't know that the Worcester had ever been there.'

For a collector, her unconcern was baffling.

'I believe it was Japanese in style,' said Cribb.

'Yes. One of Hadley's pieces. I gave a description to the constable.'

'Thank you, ma'am. I've got a note of it.'

'There are lots of them about, you know. I can find a replacement if I want one, and I'm not sure whether I do.'

'Was it on display here on the evening when you had

the seance with Sir Hartley Bratt and his family and Dr Probert?'

'Oh, yes. I asked Mr Brand whether it was safe to keep the vases out during the seance. One frequently hears of articles being moved by the spirits – poltergeists do such things, you know. But Mr Brand assured me that the collection would be safe. I could see that he had a proper respect for my bits of crockery, because he couldn't resist handling some of them as we were talking. That is the way they affect a man of taste. You need not hesitate to do the same.'

'My thanks, ma'am,' said Cribb, retaining a firm grip on the edge of the table behind him. 'If I may, I'd like to put a question to you that you might consider impertinent.'

'I don't expect I shall,' said Miss Crush, with an encouraging smile.

'Very well. How much did you pay Mr Brand for his services as a medium?'

'His fee was ten guineas. I gave him a little extra because it was such a productive seance. Lady Bratt saw a spirit hand, you know.'

'And were you satisfied that all the phenomena were genuine?'

'Absolutely, Sergeant. Well, I will admit that Lady Bratt is an excitable person and might have been mistaken about the hand, but we *all* felt the table move and heard the tapping.'

'It feels a pretty solid piece of furniture to me,' said Cribb, turning to examine the understructure. He stopped, peered underneath and was so unprepared for what he saw that he rapped his head on the underside of the table. 'God help us, ma'am, there's a man under here!'

'I know,' said Miss Crush, matter-of-factly. 'You may come out now, Mr Strathmore.'

Strathmore! The man from the Life After Death Society.

He emerged slowly on all fours like an exhibit at the zoological gardens coming out to sun itself. The brown worsted of his suit encompassed his bulk, but not without definite indications of strain from the exceptional posture. Upright, he was revealed as a short man, burly, not obese. He jammed a monocle over his right eye and said, 'There is absolutely no need to go for your truncheon, Sergeant. One had a very good reason for being where one was. I am not your burglar, I promise you. Search me if you like. All you will find are my watch, a notebook, two pencils, a magnifying glass and a tape measure.'

'I'm sure it isn't necessary, sir,' said Cribb. 'I was just a little unprepared to find—'

'A man under my table?' said Miss Crush. 'I thought of telling you when you first came in, but it is not the sort of thing a lady cares to mention the moment after a policeman is shown into her room. What constructions you might have put upon it! How was I to explain that Mr Strathmore is a distinguished investigator of spiritual phenomena who had come by appointment to inspect my table? He had just got underneath when you arrived.'

'Honorary Secretary of the Life After Death Society,' said Strathmore, pushing a visiting-card into Cribb's hand. 'Object: to investigate the claims of mediums and test them scientifically, with the ultimate intention of establishing conclusively the existence of the hereafter.'

Cribb looked up from the card. No doubt of it: the man was speaking in earnest. 'Is that what you were doing under the table?'

'But of course. One has to test for so many things – loose floorboards, hidden springs, hollow legs. Let us face the facts, Sergeant. I have carried out my duties as a member of the Society for twelve years, no less, and I have yet to find a medium who is not a fraud or a charlatan. My job is to expose such people, eliminate them, you see. I am quite ruthless in uncovering their hocus-pocus, but as a seeker after truth, I must be. It is the only certain way of discovering someone who genuinely has the power.'

'You're still looking for such a person after twelve years?'

'I am.' Strathmore held up his right forefinger in the manner of one of the prophets of old. 'Fifteen years ago, before the Society was formed, there was a man who may just conceivably have had that gift for which we search. His name was Daniel Home. In seance after seance he produced phenomena that astonished and convinced his sitters. He repeated the effects in laboratory conditions for no less a scientist than Mr William Crookes. Oh, unbelievable things! Imagine the scene in the laboratory when Crookes presented Home with a new accordion, bought that morning in Conduit Street. The medium held one end of it at arm's length, while an unseen power played a plaintive tune on the other.'

'There was a famous levitation incident, too,' contributed Miss Crush, 'when Home floated horizontally out of one window at Ashley House and in through another in the presence of two peers of the realm and an army officer.'

'I've heard that story, ma'am,' said Cribb. 'I also seem to remember an action at law a few years ago concerning thirty thousand pounds' worth of mortgage securities that

Mr Home and his spirits had managed to persuade a rich widow to transfer to him. His seances weren't so popular with the well-to-do after that.'

'You *are* well-informed,' said Miss Crush, more in the tone of a rebuff than a compliment.

'It hasn't changed the opinion of William Crookes,' said Strathmore, icily.

'I'm glad to hear it, sir. It'd be a dull world if all of us were sceptics. Personally I'm looking forward to meeting young Brand.'

'You're going to *meet* him?' said Miss Crush, in horror. 'Sergeant, I don't think that is wise.'

'Why not, ma'am? He doesn't frighten me.'

'No, but you will frighten him. He is such a delicate young man. So impressionable. And his heart is not strong, you know. I should hate him to think he is under suspicion of removing that wretched vase from my house. The shock might be enough to put out the spiritual fire in the boy.'

'Good gracious, yes,' said Strathmore. 'We can't let a piece of porcelain spoil a chance of unravelling the mystery of the Universe.'

'Ah, but there's the matter of another mystery as well, sir. A missing *Nymph and Satyrs*. Property of your friend, Dr Probert. I'm bound to ask Mr Brand if he can help me over that. I'll treat him gentle, ma'am. Rest assured of that. I've heard so much about him that I'd rather like to sit in on one of his seances myself.'

'That could be arranged, I'm sure,' said Miss Crush. 'One simply wishes to spare him the embarrassment of questions from the police.'

'He's subject to the law, like any one of us, ma'am,' said Cribb solemnly.

'Oh dear, this is very upsetting,' said Miss Crush. 'It might discourage him from ever coming here again, or going to Dr Probert's. I think I must insist that you forget about the missing vase, Sergeant.'

'Drop the investigation, d'you mean?' said Cribb in disbelief.

'Call the hounds off, so to speak,' Strathmore explained, putting a hand on Cribb's shoulder.

'Can't do that, sir.'

'Why ever not?'

'It's a criminal matter. The thief who took the vase might take something else from another member of the public. Someone made off with Dr Probert's nymph, after all. No, I shall need to talk to Mr Brand, same as I've talked to you. I haven't been uncivil, have I?'

'Quite the reverse, Sergeant,' answered Miss Crush, pulling open the sideboard door. 'I was about to offer you a sherry.'

'Never touch it, thank you, ma'am.'

'Something stronger, perhaps?'

'No, ma'am. I don't get on with spirits.' He paused. 'Of the alcoholic sort, that is.'

Strathmore's mouth formed stiffly into the shape of a smile. 'Spirits. Ah ha! You're a sharp one, Sergeant, very sharp.'

Cribb smiled back. It was the confident smile of a man in control. These people would laugh at any quip he made, however excruciating, because they wanted his co-operation over the matter of Brand. It would be dereliction of duty not to press his advantage. 'Not sharp enough, I'm afraid, sir.'

Strathmore pricked up the eyebrow that was not holding

his monocle in place. 'What do you mean by that, Sergeant?'

'Well, sir, a detective should know what's going on. When I walked in here just now I had not the slightest suspicion that you were under the table. Dr Probert's table I could understand, but not Miss Crush's.'

'Ah. You mean that I was present at the seance which took place at Richmond, but you had not connected me with this good lady's house?'

'Exactly.'

'The explanation is quite simple,' said Strathmore. 'Dr Probert's party was the first opportunity one had of seeing young Brand at the table and one was sufficiently impressed by the phenomena he produced to make further investigations. Miss Crush most kindly proposed a visit to her house to examine the scene of the previous seance, where the spirit hand was alleged to have materialized. Only when we have eliminated every possibility of trickery and deception can we begin to take a medium seriously, you see.'

'And have you discovered anything suspicious?'

'Nothing at all. The table is perfectly in order, as was Dr Probert's. One hesitates to say it, but I think we may have found—'

'A second Home, sir?'

'It would be premature to say as much as that, Sergeant. It is sufficient for the moment to state that one has found nothing to suggest that Mr Brand is fraudulent. And that, I may say, is remarkable. You would be surprised how blatant the deceptions are that the majority of so-called mediums practise on the public. I have myself seen an apparition materialize in the drawing-room two streets

41

away from here which when one unexpectedly turned up the gas was all too tangibly revealed as a young woman dressed in a cheesecloth shift with – pardon my explicit language, Miss Crush – the unmistakable outlines of a corset underneath.'

'The hussy!' whispered Miss Crush.

'So you see that my Society has to be unceasingly vigilant,' said Strathmore, folding his arms.

'I expect you made a full inspection of Dr Probert's house,' said Cribb.

'Not the whole of the house, Sergeant. Merely the room where the seance took place.'

'I see. Dr Probert didn't show you his picture-gallery then?'

'He most certainly did not.' It was difficult to tell from Strathmore's emphasis whether he was scandalized at the suggestion that he might be interested in looking at Dr Probert's naked ladies, or whether he thought the question sought to implicate him in the theft of the Etty.

'But I expect you stayed behind after Mr Brand had left?' insisted Cribb.

'Of course. It was my duty as an investigator to look under the table.'

'I stayed afterwards, too,' said Miss Crush. 'I was far too excited by what I had seen to go home immediately. Miss Alice Probert arranged for some cocoa to be served, as a nightcap, she said. It had a very calming effect on the nerves.'

'I drink it myself, ma'am. So Mr Brand left the house at what time, would you say?'

'Half past ten,' said Strathmore. 'I keep a meticulous record of every seance I attend. He had a hansom waiting for him.'

'At what time did you leave, sir?'

'It was twenty minutes to twelve. I left a few minutes after Miss Crush. Mr Nye, Miss Probert's fiancé, had very decently gone out to call carriages for us.'

Cribb turned to Miss Crush. 'So Mr Brand left at least an hour before you did, ma'am, and when you got home you discovered that your vase was missing. Now do you understand why I must put some questions to him?'

4

To the promised land; join those who, Thursday next,
Meant to meet Shakespeare;

The notices outside the Store Street Hall in Bedford Square
were persuasively worded:

THE WORLD BEHIND THE VEIL

A Public Address and Lantern Show upon the Revelations
of the Life to Come vouchsafed in recent years to such
celebrated mediums as Mr D. D. Home, Mr Stainton Moses,
Miss Florence Cook and the Speaker himself,

Professor Eustace Quayle

in which Genuine Spirit Photographs will be projected on to
a screen Eight Feet Square, and introducing the remarkable
young medium,

Mr Peter Brand

whose seances at a number of distinguished houses in

London of recent weeks have been attended by the most
sensational phenomena.
Seating for 600 persons
Admission Threepence. Gallery Twopence.
Thursday November 12th, 1885, at 7.30 p.m.

Inside, as the converted and the curious assembled, a harmonium was playing *Who are these, like stars appearing*, and towards the back of the hall Constable Thackeray was reporting confidentially to Sergeant Cribb, on the results of his visits to police stations in Richmond and Belgravia.

'I might say, Sarge, that I got a pretty cool reception at both places. The local blokes think they was perfectly capable of catching the thief, and I don't blame 'em.'

'Nor I,' said Cribb, 'but the plain fact is that we're accountable to Jowett, and if I were you I wouldn't question the whys and wherefores of it. He's in thick with Dr Probert, and Probert wants it handled by the Yard and that's the end of it. He's coming tonight, by the way.'

'Dr Probert?'

'Inspector Jowett. Better get your feet off the seat in front and try to look a credit to the Force. Did you get anything of interest from B Division?'

Thackeray took out his notebook and consulted it discreetly under cover of his overcoat. 'October 31st. Theft of Royal Worcester vase, Hereafter House, 92, Eaton Square, Belgravia. Property of Miss Laetitia Crush.'

Cribb raised an eyebrow. 'Lettie, eh? Suits her. Carry on.'

'Estimated value thirty pounds,' continued Thackeray. 'Japanese in style, made by one James Hadley—'

'Cut the description,' ordered Cribb. 'What about the means of entry?'

'A glass pane nine inches by eleven was broken in the rear door,' read Thackeray. 'It appears to have been accomplished with a brick which was found nearby. The glass fell on to a piece of coconut matting, and the servants heard nothing.'

'Clumsy, even so,' said Cribb.

'Yes, Sarge, particularly as there was a window with a broken sashcord not ten yards away. He could have got through there, easy.'

'What about the Richmond job?' said Cribb. 'How does the method of entry compare?'

'Oh, that was uncommon crude as well, Sarge.' Thackeray thumbed the pages of his notebook to check the damage inflicted on Dr Probert's property. 'The felon made a number of unsuccessful attempts to prise the bars off the pantry-window with a pick-handle before seizing on the notion of using it in conjunction with a thong. He made a shocking mess of the pantry, climbing in, too. Knocked over a tin of Bath Olivers and scattered a packet of pearl barley all over the floor. We're not exactly dealing with a Charlie Peace, Sarge. That's what so infuriates the bobbies on the spot. They reckon they could run the man to ground in a matter of hours, given the chance. It's obviously someone who knew the nights when Miss Crush was out at Dr Probert's, and Dr Probert was giving his lecture at University College Hospital. A dabbler in this table-tapping nonsense and pretty poor hand as a burglar.'

'Inspector Jowett,' said Cribb.

'Eh?' ejaculated Thackeray.

'Good evening, Officers,' said Jowett, at his side. 'You don't mind if I join you? I think the lecture is about to commence.' He just had time to take the seat on Cribb's other side. The harmonium strains gave way to polite applause as the chairman for the evening stepped out from behind a tub of pampas grass to occupy the centre of the stage.

'Ladies and gentlemen, it is my privilege tonight . . .' he began.

'This promises to be instructive,' said Jowett in Cribb's ear. 'Professor Quayle has had his palms on the tables of some of the best addresses in London. He stepped into D. D. Home's shoes in the seventies. In demand everywhere. Now it looks as if young Brand is ready to eclipse him. Decent of Quayle to include the boy in his lecture.'

Cribb gave an affirmative grunt. He was getting used to hearing mediums discussed as if they were tenors or fiddle-players. It didn't matter to the well-to-do whether there was anything in spiritualism or not; mediums were drawing-room entertainers, as ready to be hired for an evening as the latest velvet-voiced Italian over for the season at Covent Garden.

'. . . I give you Professor Eustace Quayle,' concluded the chairman, neatly stepping back behind the pampas grass.

The professor, a man of commanding height and total baldness, advanced to the lectern, propped his elbows on it and leaned forward until his head and shoulders loomed over the front rows like a figurehead. 'Who will deny that there are visitors from the Other Side in this place tonight?' he demanded in a voice that rang through the hall. There was not a whisper from the audience as he cast his eyes

47

challengingly along their stunned rows. It was not notably his baldness that intimidated, nor the extreme hollowness of his cheeks. It was the intensity of his eyes, so deep-set as to be fathomless under the gas-burners, and topped by a prodigious growth of eyebrow. 'They are everywhere about us, are they not?' he continued, with a glance which seemed to take in the back rows.

Thackeray shifted in his seat, turned slightly and found himself eye to anxious eye with his neighbour, a grey-haired lady in a racoon fur hat.

'Invisible presences,' said Professor Quayle. 'The unseen spirits of the departed. Unseen? Oh, I have seen them, my friends, seen them and spoken with them, as any of you may do if you wish. Tonight I shall show you photographic plates that will satisfy the most sceptical among you. But I am not here to persuade you that beings exist outside the material world. You are free agents. You think, and act upon the promptings of your thoughts, and we call the faculty within you that determines those thoughts your inner being, your soul, your spirit. I tell you, friends, that the spirits that a medium makes contact with are nothing but the souls of men and women like yourselves extracted from their envelope of gross, terrestrial matter.'

'Isn't that Dr Probert there, second row from the front and two from the end?' Jowett unexpectedly asked Cribb.

'You're right, sir! And Miss Crush sitting next to him.'

'Ah, you've met the lady already. She was gratified to learn that Scotland Yard are on the track of her stolen vase, no doubt.'

'That wasn't my impression, sir.'

'No?' Inspector Jowett turned in surprise.

On the platform, the professor had finished talking about the spirits in the hall and had reached the less disturbing matter of his conversations with famous historical personages from St Peter onwards.

Cribb waited till the roll had passed by way of Julius Caesar and William Shakespeare to George Washington.

'Miss Crush would like us to abandon the case, sir. Says she doesn't mind about the vase.'

'Good Lord!' said Jowett loudly.

The man on his left frowned and leaned forward in an attitude plainly conveying that if he *had* to listen to blasphemies he preferred them to come from the platform.

'I think she doesn't want to upset the people she knows, sir. It's not worth the price of the missing vase to have her spiritualistic friends investigated.'

'Understandable, I will admit, but quite impossible. You told her that you have your job to do, I hope?'

'Left her in no doubt at all, sir.'

Below, the professor quoted from a conversation he had recently had with Napoleon, '"March forward, children! You do not need the aid of bayonets to sustain your cause. Truth is more powerful than armies, fleets, cannon and grape-shot."'

'Hear, hear,' someone shouted in the middle of the hall, and there was a nervous burst of applause in which Miss Crush could be seen to be joining energetically.

'I trust you didn't threaten the lady,' said Jowett. 'People of her class aren't accustomed to bullying methods, you know. To be frank, I was somewhat disturbed by something Dr Probert repeated to me this afternoon, that you were planning to "put the screws on Miss Crush". That's not the

49

way we conduct our investigations is it, Sergeant – not where people of refinement are concerned?'

'Slip of the tongue, sir. Nothing sinister intended.'

'I can vouch for that, sir,' added Thackeray, leaning forward to catch Jowett's eyes.

'Good God! I hope *you* weren't there,' said the inspector as if that would have confirmed his worst suspicions of police brutality.

Remarkable as they were, Professor Quayle's conversations with the great would undoubtedly have taken a stronger grip on the attention of the audience if they had been extensively edited. There was a disappointing sameness about them. There seemed to be a conspiracy on the Other Side to give nothing away about the life hereafter. The communications consisted in the main of expressions of goodwill and exhortations to keep getting in touch, not helped by the professor's delivery, which was strongly reminiscent of the Best Man at a wedding reception reading out the messages from absent guests. When Lord Beaconsfield was reached, and the audience realized that his recent decease almost certainly made him last on the list, an unmistakable sensation of relief spread through the hall.

It was a critical phase in the proceedings. The moment the references to primroses and the Conservative party were rounded off with applause, a strong injection of interest was wanted if the lecture was to be kept alive. Happily it was available. 'At this juncture, ladies and gentlemen,' said the professor, 'I beg leave to introduce a young medium whose seances in recent weeks have been attended by phenomena of a most exceptional character and variety – so exceptional, in fact, that he is rapidly becoming the talk of the metropolis. Noises and rappings under a table in the suburbs are nothing new, but what do you say to the materialization of a spirit hand in Kensington, the levitation of the entire furniture of a room in Hampstead and the writing of a message from the late Duke of Wellington in a private house in Camberwell – writing, I may say, that has been verified as authentic by the foremost graphologist in London? These are examples chosen at random to convey an impression of the scope of this young man's powers – or rather, his faculty for concentrating the powers of the spirits to produce such prodigious phenomena. Ladies and gentlemen, he is young and unused to the public platform, but he has generously consented to appear beside me here tonight – Mr Peter Brand.'

For a novice, Peter Brand had a nice sense of timing. There was sufficient delay in his appearance for a germ of anxiety to flit momentarily into the minds of the audience. Then he stepped round the pampas grass, bowed humbly and shook Quayle's hand. He was notably shorter than the professor, slightly built and pale of face, with a misty uncertainty in his eyes likely to cause maternal flutterings in every bosom in the hall. He had long, black hair and wore a navy blue velveteen suit and a white cravat.

'He doesn't *look* like Charlie Peace,' Cribb remarked to Thackeray. 'What do you think?'

'Shifty little beggar, Sarge. I wouldn't trust him.'

'You will appreciate, ladies and gentlemen, that this is not the occasion for a seance,' announced Professor Quayle, 'and Mr Brand is not one of those so-called mediums who produce unusual effects for no better reason than to demonstrate their powers. Like me, he respects his mediumship as a gift from the Almighty, and he employs it only in humility and out of respect for the souls of those who have gone before on the Great Journey, but care to linger awhile and offer comfort to we who follow.'

'At ten guineas a time,' muttered Cribb.

'Nevertheless, it may be that some of the unseen audience who are in this hall with us tonight have messages to convey to the living. And therefore in all humility Mr Brand has agreed to put his gift at their disposal. Lest there are those among you who would not wish to contact their dear ones in the forum of an open meeting, he undertakes to convey messages only to those who signify their willingness by placing some small personal article in one of the envelopes we shall presently provide, and inscribing their names in pencil on the outside.'

'If you please,' called a voice towards the front, and an attendant hurried over with a large brown envelope.

'Miss Crush,' Thackeray declared in a disillusioned voice. 'I reckon they'll all be people he knows, Sarge.'

'They needn't be,' said Cribb. 'What have you got in your pocket?'

'Glory! Only my darbies—'

'Just the thing. Lean across and call for an envelope.'

So Thackeray, not for the first time, found himself elbowed into the front line by Sergeant Cribb.

'Very good,' the professor presently said. 'We now have four envelopes containing personal articles belonging to members of the audience. We shall see whether any of them evokes a response from the Other Side. Will you take this one first, Mr Brand? The name on the envelope is Miss L. Crush.'

'Miss Crush,' repeated Brand.

'Speak up, sir,' requested someone at the rear of the hall.

Brand nodded an acknowledgement, and put his hand in the envelope. 'It is a glove,' he said in a more carrying voice, and held it out for everyone to confirm the fact. 'If you will bear with me . . .' He put his other hand to his forehead and closed his eyes.

The audience waited breathlessly.

'Do you have a residence in Belgravia, Miss Crush?' he asked without opening his eyes.

'Yes, yes, I do,' called Miss Crush from her place in the second row, as triumphantly as if this information alone confirmed the Life Everlasting.

'Then there is something coming through for you from one of an older generation. A male person. An uncle. The name is difficult. Something like . . .' His voice tailed off.

'Walter,' said Miss Crush helpfully.

'Yes, that is his name. Your Uncle Walter, who passed over not long ago. Perhaps a year ago.'

'Perfectly right!' said Miss Crush, looking to right and left to share her enthusiasm with the audience.

'He wishes you to know that he remembers many years ago taking you to the Great Exhibition at the Crystal Palace. Is that correct?'

'Absolutely!' cried Miss Crush, adding, 'I was no more than a child, of course.'

'He sends you a message. It is to say that the Great Exhibition where he is now is even more magnificent. Does that make sense to you?'

'Infinite sense,' said Miss Crush. 'Thank you.' There were appreciative murmurs all round the hall.

The next two envelopes contained a pocket-book and a silver watch respectively. The owners were plainly delighted by the despatches that reached them from the Other Side. Brand was growing in confidence. 'May I have the last envelope, if you please? Thank you. It feels somewhat heavier than the others. What did you say the name on the outside is, Professor? E. Thackeray? May I see where Mr Thackeray is situated in the auditorium?'

'On your feet,' said Cribb to his assistant.

'Do you think this is wise, Sergeant?' asked Jowett.

'We'll shortly see, sir.'

'Thank you, Mr Thackeray,' said Brand. He put his hand in the envelope and drew it out. 'What do we have here?'

'Handcuffs!' cried someone at the front. The word was taken up and passed from row to row in a buzz of disbelief. Those towards the back craned to see for themselves. Perhaps only Sergeant Cribb of all the audience was not studying the object dangling from Peter Brand's hand, but the expression on his face. The medium was clearly unable to cope with this development.

Professor Quayle stepped to the edge of the platform and addressed Thackeray: 'Is this intended as some form of practical joke, sir, because if it is I think the audience would wish me to state that it is in arrant bad taste?'

'Lord, no,' said Thackeray in an injured voice. 'It was the only thing I had in my pocket except my notebook and it's more than my job's worth to part with that.'

'You are a policeman?'

'That's right, sir,' said Thackeray amiably.

'A policeman out of uniform?'

'Right again, sir,' said Thackeray, in the encouraging tone the other volunteers in the audience had used to respond to accurate assumptions from the platform.

'But you are prepared for all emergencies?'

'Every one, sir.'

'That would account for the handcuffs, then,' said Professor Quayle, with a slight note of conciliation in his voice. 'I suggest that what you failed to appreciate, Officer, is that a pair of handcuffs cannot be described as a personal article, except possibly by someone of your own avocation. An article of that sort is not likely to evoke a response from the Ones Above, you see. They wouldn't think of handcuffs as personal.'

'There's some in the Other Place that might, sir,' said Thackeray.

It was a retort that delighted the audience and gave Cribb the opportunity of restoring Thackeray firmly in his seat.

Quayle, for his part, seemed content to close the dialogue. 'With the permission of our well-connected policeman friend, I shall move on to other matters, ladies and gentlemen. If the attendants will kindly turn down the gas and bring forward the magic lantern, we shall proceed to the spirit photographs, which I am confident will remove any doubts you may still have left about the existence of the supernatural.'

The lantern, already ignited and with a powerful head of paraffin-fumes issuing from its funnel, was conveyed along the central aisle on a trolley and pointed at a large white screen which the professor unrolled from somewhere above the centre of the platform. The lights were lowered and the image of a young woman seated in a tall-backed chair was projected on to the screen. Anyone of a nervous disposition must have been reassured by the substantial form of the sitter.

'This is a photographic plate of the medium, Miss Georgina Houghton, taken at the studio of the spirit photographer, Mr Frederick Hudson,' announced Quayle. 'You will observe that there is nothing remarkable about it. Now examine this one, taken a few minutes after.'

Miss Houghton on her chair was moved rapidly leftwards and replaced on the screen by another picture of herself, identically posed. This time a faceless figure draped in white stood behind the chair. A general in-drawing of breath was audible all over the hall.

'If anyone would care to see it, I can produce an affidavit sworn by Miss Houghton and Mr Hudson that no other mortal being was present in the studio when these pictures were taken,' said the professor. 'How then are we to account for the second figure? Is it the result of some quirk of the photographic process – a faulty plate, perhaps, or the intrusion of light into the camera? If that is what you suspect, then I invite you to look at the next plate.'

It was an invitation Cribb was sorry to refuse, but something he had noticed made it quite impossible for him or Thackeray to stay any longer. Mr Peter Brand had taken advantage of the darkness to quit the platform and make for an exit at the side of the hall. 'Matter to attend to, sir,' Cribb whispered to Jowett, then jabbed Thackeray in the ribs and piloted him to the end of the row, remarking as they stumbled over knees, feet and umbrellas that the paraffin-fumes were insufferable.

They reached the door some ten seconds after Brand had gone through. He was walking briskly up Store Street in the direction of Tottenham Court Road. 'One moment, sir!' Cribb shouted after him. Brand did not look round.

'I'll stop the blighter,' said Thackeray, starting to run.

'No violence, Constable!' cautioned Cribb.

Thackeray knew better than to disobey an order. If the manner in which he caught Peter Brand by the shoulder, twisted his arm into a half-Nelson and jammed him against a convenient lamp-post so that the breath erupted from his lungs in a great gasp, suggested anything but a routine request to co-operate with the Force, then thirty years' service had gone for naught.

'Perishing cold night, Mr Brand,' remarked Cribb when he drew level with them. 'This ain't the time of year to be out without a hat and coat. Left 'em behind in the hall, did you? You'll pardon us for coming after you. We were hoping for a few minutes of your time. Release the gentleman's arm, Thackeray. I think he understands us. Let's all walk peaceably back to the hall and find ourselves a quiet room for a spot of conversation.'

'Pity about the spirit photographs,' Cribb resumed, when the three of them were installed in the caretaker's office. 'It isn't every day you get the chance of seeing apparitions, but then I suppose you've seen the show before, Mr Brand?'

If it were possible, the young medium looked paler and more vulnerable than he had on the platform. He said nothing.

'Some say it's trickery, of course,' continued Cribb. 'Doctored plates and double exposures. Perhaps you didn't approve of the photographs, and walked out to register your protest?'

Whether Cribb was correct in this assumption or not, Brand was disinclined by now to register anything at all.

'Personally I have another theory,' said Cribb. 'It could have been the sight of Thackeray's handcuffs that upset you. Shabby trick to play on a sensitive man, particularly if he's done anything to be ashamed of. I'm not suggesting that you have, sir. It's Thackeray that ought to be ashamed, not you. He positively stopped you in the middle of your act, didn't he?'

'It ain't an act,' said Brand unexpectedly.

'My mistake, sir. Unfortunate word.'

'I didn't want to parade on a blooming platform,' Brand went on, in a cockney accent difficult to reconcile with extra-sensory powers. 'Quayle put me up to it. 'E says I've got to get my name before the public, and 'e's such a regular pal that I can't refuse 'im. Took me in, 'e did, and taught me 'ow to get in touch. It's a gift, you know, but you've still got to learn 'ow to 'andle it.'

'I'm sure,' said Cribb. 'I should think it changed your life.'

'Out of all bleeding recognition,' said Brand. 'It's taken me into some of the nobbiest 'ouses in London. Mingled with the aristocracy, I 'ave. Could never 'ave done it without the professor.'

'He sounds a very generous man. What made him do it, do you think?'

'Ah, 'e's almost lost the power, you see. Can't produce the effects no more. It takes its toll of a man as 'e gets older. When 'e found the power was going 'e started lookin' round for someone 'e could pass 'is knowledge on to.'

'And his engagement-book, I dare say,' said Cribb.

'I got some introductions through 'im, true, but I've collected a sizeable number on my own account.'

'Would Miss Crush be one of them?'

'Miss Crush?' The faintest tinge of colour rose in Brand's cheeks. 'She would, as it 'appens.'

'She's in the audience tonight, isn't she?' said Cribb. 'She was your first volunteer. To anyone who didn't know, it must have sounded quite impressive, all that stuff about Uncle what was his name?'

'Walter,' said Brand. 'Give us a chance, guvnor. Strange things 'appen to a man of my calling. If I 'ave the good fortune to spot somebody I know, I ain't so stupid as to turn me back on 'em. The old duck was pleased enough with what she 'eard, wasn't she?'

'No doubt of that,' said Cribb. 'And quite surprising too, considering her loss on the night you had the seance at Dr Probert's.'

'Loss?' repeated Brand, vacantly.

'Didn't you hear about it? A vase was taken from her house in Eaton Square.'

'Blimey! No one told me. Not the Minton?'

'You saw it, then?' said Cribb.

'Saw 'em all lined up on the sideboard. I know a nice piece of porcelain when I spot it. Are you trying to find it then? Must be worth a cool thousand. Takes years to build up the surface on them things. They do it layer by layer.'

'It wasn't the Minton that went,' explained Cribb. 'It was a Royal Worcester piece.'

'That's all right then,' said Brand. 'Bloody rubbish, that Japanese thing. What are you asking me about it for? You don't think I would want it, do you?'

'Do you have a collection yourself?'

'Blimey, no. I'm not that flush. I might be makin' a name for meself, but I 'aven't even got me own place yet. I'm sub-lettin' a room from the professor. Got no room for china, I can tell you.'

'Pictures, perhaps?' said Cribb.

'What are you gettin' at?'

'An Etty was stolen from Dr Probert's house the other night.'

'You don't say.' Brand's jaw gaped.

'That's two of your clients,' said Cribb. 'Miss Crush and Dr Probert.'

'They don't suspect *me?*' said Brand in horror.

'*They* don't. Others might.'

'What do you take me for? It's more than my career's worth to 'elp meself to clients' property. Jesus, I'm booked for another three seances at Dr Probert's. Scientific stuff. The next one's on Saturday. I'd 'ave to be off me 'ead to filch 'is pictures, wouldn't I?'

Cribb nodded. 'No question about it.' He leaned forward. 'These things that happen in the seances, Mr Brand. Spirit hands and that sort of thing. Do you actually believe in 'em yourself?'

There was a pause. Then Brand said, 'You're tryin' to trap me, Copper. I ain't obtainin' money by false pretences, if that's what you mean. My clients understand that I can't guarantee nothin' without the co-operation of the spirits. You can ask Miss Crush or Dr Probert or 'is daughter or any of 'em what they've seen and 'eard. Things 'appen

60

when I put my 'ands on a table, strange things that none of us can account for, nor control, not even them that comes from Scotland Yard. 'Ave you ever 'eard of objects being spirited away?'

'Yes, quite often,' said Thackeray, 'but we always get the blighters in the end.'

5

Would but the shade
Of the venerable dead-one just vouchsafe
A rap or tip!

Inspector Jowett gently squeezed Miss Alice Probert's
left hand, securely clasped in his right. The pressure
was delicately calculated to convey the promise of
support, nothing else. After all, he had his reputation at
the Yard to consider. The consequence of an incautious
squeeze was quite unthinkable. Yet the experience of
holding hands, for all its hazards, was not unpleasant.
And it was illuminating. Sitting here in the dark next to
Miss Probert he understood perfectly why seances were
all the rage.

His left hand was held in the unequivocal grasp of Mr
Strathmore, the spirit investigator. Strathmore was similarly
linked to Miss Crush, and the circle was completed by Peter
Brand, Dr Probert and Captain William Nye, Miss Probert's
fiancé, who very properly held her other hand. They were
seated at an oval table in the library of Dr Probert's house
in Richmond.

He had readily accepted Probert's invitation to attend
the next experiment, as it was termed. Not that he believed

in this table-turning nonsense, but if the rest of sociable London was dabbling in it, he could hardly ignore it. The one condition he had demanded of Probert was that he was not to be introduced as a detective-inspector. It was certain to excite people, and lead them to expect clever explanations of everything that happened. Explanations were not his forte; even bottom of the bill music hall magicians mystified him absolutely. No, he was quite content to be known as Mr Jowett, a civil servant with an office in Whitehall.

The preliminaries had been got over quickly: introductions, a glass of sherry in the drawing-room and then to the library. Seven chairs were already positioned round the table, which was of polished mahogany. The room was narrow and shelved to the ceiling, but the electric light, the pride of Probert's establishment, more than compensated for the sombre bindings of the books. At one end, a set of velvet curtains divided the room, to provide a recess, which the doctor used as a study.

Hearts were alleged to beat faster when the lights went out at a seance, but the moment when Probert pulled the switch had come as a distinct relief to Jowett. Young Nye, on Miss Probert's other side, had been scrutinising him in a manner decidedly antagonistic, quite unjustifiably, in his opinion. Why should he be blamed if the fellow's Intended addressed almost all her conversation to him? Alice Probert was uncommonly appealing, he was ready to admit, with natural black curls and flashing eyes and a figure he could only describe as precocious at the age of nineteen, so perhaps Nye's state of agitation was not surprising. What torment the wretched man must be suffering with the light off!

'Please feel free to engage in subdued conversation,' said Brand's voice from the darkness. He articulated each word with the care of one who had studied elocution without altogether mastering the vowel sounds. 'I like it better than a wearisome silence and so do the spirits. If at any time during the seance you feel constrained to shout something aloud, or sing at the top of your voice, or gesticulate, I urge you for your own good to give way to the impulse. Likewise, if the person next to you goes into convulsions do not be alarmed. It is quite normal. Put a supporting arm around them and let them lean against you until the fit passes.'

That was bad news for Nye! Jowett gave Alice's hand another gentle squeeze to let her know that support was available on the left.

'I've given the domestics a night off,' said Probert, in response to the call for conversation. 'Sent them out. Didn't want them making noises round the house and alarming us.'

'Where is Mama?' asked Alice.

'As far away as she can get,' said Probert. 'I gave her a volume of *Notable British Sermons* to take upstairs. Should take her mind off the goings-on down here. Have you checked the room temperature, Strathmore?'

'Sixty-eight point five degrees,' said Strathmore. 'That was five minutes ago, at half past eight.'

'Excellent. I'm sorry about the fire-screen, ladies and gentlemen, but darkness is essential. Does anyone feel anything yet? What about you, Jowett? This is your first seance, isn't it?'

'That is so. I feel nothing exceptional, I assure you.'

'Capital. And Miss Crush?'

'I begin to feel a presence,' said the voice of Miss Crush, speaking with a strange emphasis. 'The room has become colder, has it not?'

Jowett, certainly, had goose-pimples forming rapidly on the backs of his legs.

'Is there anyone wishing to get in touch?' asked Brand.

There was no response, but now the atmosphere was charged with tension. Subdued conversation had terminated for the night. The sitters waited breathlessly for Brand to put the question again.

'Please signify your presence if you are here.'

It came at once: a distinct rap on the table.

'There it is!' cried Miss Crush superfluously.

Brand was into his routine with professional slickness. 'Are you prepared to answer questions, three raps for yes and one for no?'

Three confident raps were heard.

'Are you known to any of us?'

The same.

'To our host?'

One rap.

'Miss Crush?'

Three clear raps.

'Can you give your name?'

Five raps.

'Alphabet,' said Dr Probert, who also seemed to know his seance procedures.

Brand recited the alphabet at a rate so brisk that it seemed he was determined to get to Z without being stopped, but at W there was a sharp rap on the table. He began again, and was stopped at once by a second rap.

'A,' said Dr Probert. 'W followed by A.'

'Walter!' exclaimed Miss Crush in an intuitive flash. 'Uncle Walter!'

Three loud raps confirmed the fact.

Jowett leaned forward in the darkness, trying to locate the rappings. First they seemed to come from the medium's side of the table, but the latest sounded closer at hand. He was not taken in by them, of course. There were at least a dozen ways of producing sounds of that sort without involving the spirits. Over the years, so-called mediums had confessed to everything from castanets between their knees to cracking the joints of their big toes. There was the story of a lady at a seance who had fainted when one of her companions had cracked a biscuit. It would take something more sensational than a few knockings under a table to convince a Scotland Yard man that he was in the presence of the paranormal.

Even so, the darkness evoked irrational possibilities. The senses were primed to respond to the smallest suggestion of anything irregular. It wanted all the self possession cultivated in a lifetime in the Force to keep things in their proper perspective.

'These scientific gentlemen are here to observe the phenomena of the seance,' Brand explained to the spirit of Uncle Walter. 'Are you prepared to assist us in our experiments?'

Three raps.

Jowett felt a sudden pressure from Alice Probert's hand.

'Look!' she said. 'Something is hovering over the table.'

'By Jove, yes, I can see it!' said her fiancé.

'I, too,' said Probert.

Jowett straightened up from trying to locate the source of the raps and to his intense astonishment saw the phenomenon for himself: a patch of light, the size of a small bird, fluttering three feet above the table. The luminosity was not sufficient to irradiate the faces of the sitters, but something was undeniably there, and it was animated, too. It rose and swooped, seeming to vanish at will and reappear in another position, altering its shape miraculously.

'Do you see it, Strathmore?' asked Probert.

'Quite unbelievable!' murmured the man from the Life After Death Society.

'God save us!' said Miss Crush. 'I believe it is a hand.'

Even as Jowett watched, the fluttering movement showed sufficiently for him briefly to discern the shape of a human palm with fingers and a thumb. Not a glove, not a plaster cast: no obvious artifice. An identifiable hand, detached at the wrist, stretching and clenching in a natural manner, so that the creasing of the flesh coincided with the character-istic markings of the palm. But for all its mobility, it lacked the colour of a living hand. It was not pink; it was livid, and glowing through the darkness.

'A materialization!' whispered Probert. 'I never thought I should live—'

'Nor I,' murmured Strathmore, with awe.

'It is a common enough manifestation,' said Brand composedly. 'Keep a firm hold on each other's hands and it will come down and touch us.'

As the medium spoke, Jowett saw the fingers close over the palm, which turned in the air and vanished. An instant after, there was a scream.

'It touched my cheek!' said Miss Crush.

At once Alice Probert said, 'My dress! It is tugging at my dress!'

'Is it, by Jove?' said Nye, on her other side. 'I won't have that!'

'Keep your hands on the table,' warned Brand.

'I'm not having my Alice interfered with,' said Nye determinedly.

'It's all right, William. It has stopped,' said Alice.

'Damnable behaviour, whoever it was,' said Nye.

'Uncle Walter could never resist a pretty girl,' revealed Miss Crush.

'It's a fine time to tell us that, madam, when there's a hand at liberty under the table,' said Nye. 'Do you think we ought to go any further with this, Dr Probert?'

Before anyone could comment there was a blood-curdling bellow from Nye. 'What the blazes is going on? Someone's pelting me with fruit!'

True enough, something rolled across the table and came to rest against Jowett's hand. It must have split on impact with Nye, for there was a pungent smell of orange-juice in the air.

'The spirit has got the impression that you are a hostile presence,' Brand explained. 'Try to reassure it, Captain Nye, or the experiment will be ruined.'

'Yes, play the game, William, for Heaven's sake,' added Probert.

'The Devil I will!' said Nye, unsociably.

There was the sound of another orange making contact with Nye. A third must have missed, but hit a vase of chrysanthemums on the mantelpiece behind him, for there was a sound of a vessel overturning, followed by a rapid dripping of water into the hearth.

'The spirit has left us, ladies and gentlemen,' said Brand.

'Damn you, Nye, you've ruined everything!' exclaimed

Strathmore. 'We had the eternal secret within our grasp. I've waited twelve years for this. Twelve years!'

Nye was unrepentant. 'I'm not allowing my fiancée's clothing to be interfered with in the name of science or anything else. It's unendurable! If that's the nature of your experiments, Dr Probert, sir, I demand that Alice leaves the table, and so shall I. Good God, it's like a blasted mess-night after the Colonel's left!'

'I think it might be prudent if we all left the table for an interval,' said Probert. 'I cannot see the sense in sitting here waiting for something else to be shied at Captain Nye.'

Alice, on Jowett's right, made an odd sound in her throat which he could almost have believed was a stifled giggle. She was obviously hysterical, poor child.

'You're right,' said Brand. 'The moment has passed. We *all* need to compose ourselves. After that, I shall be happy to co-operate in the second experiment you prepared, Doctor. For the present, I suggest someone turns on the light.'

Sergeant Cribb had miscalculated. He would have laid a guinea to a gooseberry that the burglary that evening would take place at Miss Crush's. He had backed his judgement by posting Thackeray behind a tree in Eaton Square for the night. It seemed so obvious: with Miss Crush out at Richmond the Minton vase was there for the taking. Too obvious, perhaps? Thackeray was going to say some strong words about that in the morning, for the plain fact was that the man Cribb suspected of the burglaries was not in Belgravia at all. He had just let himself in through the back door of Dr Probert's residence in Richmond.

Cribb had followed him there from central London. Pursued him in a cab as far as Richmond Bridge and tracked him on foot the rest of the way. He had rarely been so surprised as when the trail led clean through Kensington High Street and on to Hammersmith, Chiswick and Richmond.

And now his suspect had confidently entered Probert's house by the back door and stepped inside. What in the name of sanity were the servants doing to leave the door unlocked? Curiously, there wasn't a light on in the basement. The only lights in the house were at the front, on the ground floor, where the seance was presumably taking place, and a small window at the top, where the timid Mrs Probert must have gone for refuge.

Probert wasn't going to welcome a detective-sergeant on the premises this evening and nor was Jowett, but Cribb knew which way duty lay. Allowing his quarry half a minute to get up the back stairs to the gallery of classical subjects, he followed by the same route.

When he reached the floor of the gallery, he found that he had made a second miscalculation. The door was locked, and the man he was pursuing was nowhere within sight or hearing.

Dr Probert's Edison-Swan lamps were not only more powerful than gas; they lit the room in full brilliance the moment the switch was turned on. The sitters blinked as their optic muscles strained to adapt to the new conditions, but the discomfort was a fair exchange for a clear sight of the room. During the seance, Jowett had felt an increasing urge to check the position of the furniture and the proximity of the walls and ceiling. It was more than a mere wish to orientate himself; it was a need to reaffirm that furniture, walls and ceiling were actually there at all.

'Would anyone care for another drink?' asked Probert, breaking the uneasy silence.

'A small gin neat wouldn't come amiss, since you mention it, Doctor,' said Miss Crush.

'If I may say so,' said Strathmore, 'it would be wiser if we all refrained from further consumption of alcohol until after the second experiment, in the interests of science. I shall, of course, be writing a full report of tonight's events for the *Proceedings* of my Society. One would not wish to report that certain of the participants had indulged themselves to the extent of a sherry followed by an undiluted gin. It would tend to detract somewhat from the authority of the report.'

'You have a good point there, Strathmore,' said Probert. 'What do you say, Miss Crush?'

'Oh, a very pertinent point, Doctor. I had no idea that we might be reported in the *Proceedings*.' She smiled coyly in Strathmore's direction. 'Will you mention any of us by name, Mr Strathmore?'

'With your permission, madam, with your permission. I have a notion that my report will be read and discussed in scientific societies all over the world when the importance of what is happening here this evening is generally known.'

'Then I shall definitely forgo the gin,' declared Miss Crush.

'In that case, I think we might proceed without delay to prepare the apparatus for the second experiment. I trust that everyone is still prepared to co-operate?' Dr Probert looked speculatively round the table, leaving the eye of his prospective son-in-law till last.

Captain Nye sniffed. 'It had better be conducted in a more decent manner than events so far tonight. I won't have my fiancée put to any more embarrassment, I promise you.'

'It's quite all right, William,' Alice assured him, taking his arm.

'I'll be the judge of that,' said Nye, primly. 'I have heard of certain very disagreeable things happening in the name of spiritualism – things you in your innocence could not begin to imagine – and I refuse to be a party to them here.'

'Nothing improper happens under my roof, I assure you,' said Probert, through his teeth.

'I'm glad to have that assurance, sir, and I respect it,' Nye went on, 'but I take a less sanguine view of the probable outcome of several people of both sexes linking hands in a darkened room.'

Before Probert could reply, Peter Brand tactfully intervened. 'It isn't absolutely necessary to link hands. The spirits don't insist upon it. We do it as a safeguard against trickery. If everyone holds hands, as we did just now, you can be quite sure that no one is producing artificial phenomena. But you need not link hands for the next experiment if you prefer not to, and I don't object to the seance taking place in a subdued light, if that would ease your mind, sir. We could take away the fire-screen and sit by the natural light of the fire.'

'That sounds a promising way to preserve decorum,' said Jowett, who felt it was time he contributed something constructive to the debate. He was resigned to relinquishing Alice Probert's hand now that Nye had made such an issue of it.

'I have no objection either way,' said Miss Crush. 'Personally, I don't feel threatened by anyone present, including poor Uncle Walter.'

'Is it agreed that we continue as Mr Brand suggests, then?' asked Strathmore, as keen as Brand to resume the seance.

'Very well,' said Nye, 'but I give due notice that Alice and I shall withdraw at the first hint of anything objectionable.'

'That's agreed, then,' said Brand cheerfully. 'Perhaps you will set up the apparatus, gentlemen. I shall repair the small amount of damage that our visitor inflicted.' He went to the mantelpiece, stood the vase of chrysanthemums in its former position and gallantly withdrew his own hand-kerchief to mop up the water spilt along the ledge and in the hearth.

'That's not necessary,' said Probert. 'I can—'

'Call a servant?' said Brand. 'I thought you'd given them a night off, sir. Leave this to me and show your other guests what is behind the curtain in your study.'

It was an electric chair.

More precisely, it was a handsome oak chair carved in the Gothic style, with brass handles screwed to the arms. Wires trailed from the handles to a black box the size and shape of a shoebox, to which a thicker lead was connected on the other side and snaked across the floor and under the door.

'It is a simple electrical circuit,' Dr Probert explained to the others as they grouped round the chair. 'I am not sure how intimately you are all acquainted with the theory of electricity. This is one of the few houses in Richmond so far connected to Mr Cooper's electrical supply station in Queen's Road. I have four storage batteries in my cellar, each with a tension of 104 volts to illuminate a house, of course, so we pass the current through a transformer which reduces it to the appropriate strength. The box you see on the floor is a step-down transformer of my own design, manufactured solely for this experiment. When I presently connect the supply to the transformer it will ensure that only a mild and even current passes through. It will travel along this copper wire to the handle of the chair. A similar wire leads from the other handle back to the transformer, so that when the handles are linked by a conducting agent an electrical circuit is formed!'

'And Mr Brand is to be our conductor!' cried Miss Crush delightedly. 'What an ingenious idea! If he takes his hands off the chair the circuit will be broken.'

'But is it quite safe?' asked Alice anxiously.

'Oh, perfectly, my dear,' her father answered. 'The current passing through him will be very mild, you see – a mere fraction of an ampere. The transformer steps down the electromotive force from the storage batteries to just twenty volts. But as an extra precaution we have thought of a further modification. It is this.' He tapped a squat, metal instrument with a glass face, behind which a numbered dial was marked. 'This is a galvanometer. It measures the strength of electricity which passes through it. I am going to introduce it into the circuit by connecting it to this wire which trails from the right arm of the chair. The wire is long enough uncoiled to enable us to have the galvanometer with us on the other side of the curtain. Mr Brand will sit here holding the chair-handles and we shall know from the instrument whether he breaks the contact for so much as a fraction of a second.'

'Bravo!' said Miss Crush. 'What splendid reading it will

make in Mr Strathmore's report! I can visualize it already – *The Medium who Stood the Test of Electrical Science.*'

'The *Proceedings* is a professional journal, madam, not a penny newspaper,' said Strathmore, his monocle gleaming.

'Frankly, it seems to me that you're going to excessive lengths to make sure that the fellow's hands stay on the chair,' said Nye, voicing the thought that was crossing Jowett's mind. 'Wouldn't it be simpler to have a couple of us watching him instead of a confounded galvanometer on the other side of a curtain?'

'It would indeed,' said Probert, 'but it would certainly destroy the experiment. Mr Brand has been persuaded this evening to attempt the ultimate feat in the repertoire of spiritualism. It calls for a quite exceptional summoning of the powers at his disposal. He is going to pass into a state of total trance, and for this he requires a situation in which he is physically isolated. There are practical reasons for this: a medium completely in trance is in a singularly vulnerable state; he has, in effect, broken contact with the world, and any noise or interruption, however accidental, must come as a severe shock. Mr Brand will not mind my confiding to you that although he is no invalid, his constitution is not of the strongest. He has a condition known to the layman as a murmuring heart – not a serious handicap in normal circumstances, but one which could conceivably be complicated by a sudden shock. The few mediums who have attempted what Mr Brand is to try for the benefit of science this evening have always worked from a detached room or a specially constructed cabinet which insulates them from unpredictable shocks. We should be grateful that Mr Brand is prepared not only to attempt this experiment, but to submit to the intrusion of our electrical wires.'

'I am profoundly grateful,' murmured Miss Crush.

'I'm sure you are, ma'am. And I have no doubt that the entire scientific world will share your sentiment if the experiment is successful.'

'What *is* the object of the experiment, then, for Heaven's sake?' demanded Nye.

'The object, William, is to produce, in scientifically controlled conditions, the total manifestation of a spirit.'

6

'Did you detect a cheat here? Wait! Let's see!
Just an experiment first, for candour's sake!'

They had asked Inspector Jowett to take the galvano-meter readings. There was sufficient light at the fireside to observe the tremors of the needle, and he squatted by the instrument with Strathmore at his side noting the information in a pocket-book. In different circumstances it would have pleased him to be invited to play an active part in such a crucial experiment. Tonight he had reservations.

Early in the evening he had begun to ponder the reason for his presence at the seance. On accepting Probert's invitation to attend he had not given it a second thought. It was a mark of gratitude, a return for the small service he had rendered the doctor by arranging that Scotland Yard took over the burglary investigation.

But was it only that? As the scientific purpose of the evening had become increasingly clear, he had started to wonder whether there was not some other reason for his presence there; you did not, after all, select a team of scientific investigators on a social basis. Wonder had grown into something more disturbing when Strathmore had talked of publishing his findings in the *Proceedings* of the

Life After Death Society. People reading extraordinary claims in scientific reports quite properly took an interest in the status and integrity of those who participated. There could scarcely be a more convincing endorsement than the presence of a detective-inspector of the Metropolitan Police.

It was worrying, confoundedly worrying. For whilst Probert had given his word to say nothing during the evening about the occupation and rank of his visitor from Whitehall, no promise had been given or requested to keep it confidential afterwards. In his report, Strathmore would expect to list the names and professions of all the witnesses, and very impressive they would appear: two ladies well known in social circles of Richmond and Kensington, two distinguished men of medicine, an army officer and . . . a detective-inspector of police. How Scotland Yard would receive the information that one of its senior detectives had seen a spirit hand was not to be imagined. And that was the less startling item on the evening's agenda! Was it too much to hope that Uncle Walter's spirit might have returned to the Other Side in a fit of pique?

The needle was steady at a reading of 205. For the purpose of the experiment the electric light had been disconnected, and the final preparations had taken place by candlelight. Probert had gone to some trouble to ensure that a good contact was made with the medium's hands, by wrapping small squares of lint soaked in a saline solution round the handles of the chair. Other members of the party had been invited to sit in the chair and test the sensation of the electrical current. Miss Crush pronounced it 'agreeably stimulating, like the tingle of champagne'; Strathmore found it 'unobjectionable'; and Captain Nye said he could not feel anything at all. Before Brand took his place in the chair he agreed to be searched to make certain he had nothing concealed that might be used to fake a materialization. At length everyone retired to the main part of the room, the curtain was drawn and the candles extinguished.

Five minutes passed without anything but a series of small snorts and sighs from Nye to register his impatience with the whole business.

'Perhaps it would help if we all linked hands again,' suggested Miss Crush. 'Speaking personally, I find that it brings my thoughts more into harmony with other members of the circle.'

'We've been into that already, madam,' said Strathmore, before Nye had a chance to explode. 'The medium says it isn't necessary. Besides, Jowett and I have got to be over here with the galvanometer. Ah, there's a movement!'

'A drop to 196,' said Jowett.

'And that is at 10.20 p.m.,' said Strathmore, writing it down.

'He must have altered his position slightly,' explained Probert. 'The instrument is sensitive to the smallest fluctuations in the strength of the contact.'

'I expect he has gone more deeply into trance,' said Miss Crush.

The flickering illumination provided by the fire might have eased Captain Nye's doubts about the propriety of the proceedings, but it put the sitters' nerves to the test more rigorously, if anything, than pitch darkness. Their own shadows leapt about the shelves and walls of the library. Because the effect was unpredictable it was impossible to ignore. The sudden movement caught in the corner of

one's eye was almost certainly a shadow on the curtain –
almost, but how could anyone be sure?

'Here's a change. 188,' reported Jowett.

'At 10.25 p.m.,' said Strathmore.

A log shifted in the grate. There was a sharp in-drawing
of breath from somebody.

'Compose yourselves,' cautioned Probert. 'If we all
remain in control there is nothing to fear.'

Miss Crush at once raised her right hand with forefinger
erect as if she was about to admonish her host. Instead she
held it poised in front of her, her several rings glinting
fiercely. After several seconds she announced, 'I divine a
presence. It is the same sensation as before, a chilling of
the atmosphere. Oh yes, I am sure of it. There is a visitor
in the room with us now.'

Strathmore accepted this information with scientific
detachment. 'A drop in temperature, you say? We should
have taken thermometer readings, Probert. It would have
provided more evidence for my report. Next time—'

'Please do not be alarmed, anyone, but I am quite sure
that a hand is stroking my hair,' said Alice Probert suddenly.
'It is quite all right, William. It means no harm. If everyone
will only keep calm . . . It wants to come among us.'

'The galvanometer is steady at 188,' said Jowett in a low
voice. *Someone* had to remind the ladies to keep the observations on a scientific level. Heavens, if he was to be
deprived by tonight's doings of the chance of promotion
to chief-inspector, it warranted something more sensational
than a draught through Alice Probert's hair!

As if in response to his thought, there was an astonishing
development from behind the curtain, the sound of something, some *being* walking across the carpet.

The needle of the galvanometer had not moved from 188.

'God save us all!' cried Miss Crush.

From behind the curtain a voice shouted, 'What's the bloody game?'

'It must be a spirit,' Miss Crush declared in a stage whisper. 'That is not the way Mr Brand speaks.'

Certainly the outburst had lacked the painstaking articulation of Brand's utterances earlier in the evening.

The footsteps recrossed the study, moving more quickly. The galvanometer had risen to 196.

'Should someone look behind the curtain?' asked Alice.

'It's a bloody liberty!' said the voice.

'I think we would be justified in doing so,' said Dr Probert. 'Strathmore, you are nearest. Would you be so kind?'

The representative from the Life After Death Society advanced gingerly to the curtain and pulled it far enough aside to look through. 'Is everything quite in order, Mr Brand?'

'No it ain't,' said the medium, and the voice was now recognizable as his. 'Fetch Dr Probert in 'ere quick.'

Probert was on his feet in a moment and bustled past Strathmore into the study. His haste was unfortunate. 'Damn! I've kicked over the blasted bowl of salt solution. Light a candle, someone, for God's sake, and bring it in here.'

Strathmore located a candle on the mantelpiece, lighted it from the fire and took it to Probert. Peter Brand was seated gripping the chair-handles as they had left him, except that his appearance bore signs of his recent state of trance, his hair dishevelled from contact with the chair-back, jacket collar turned up and trousers, with handkerchief half hanging from them, creased concertina-fashion where he had slipped down in the chair.

There was no other person in the study with him.

'What are you tryin' to do to me, for Christ's sake?' he demanded of Probert, all affectation sunk without trace. 'You told me this was science. A bleedin' experiment. I come in good faith and what 'appens? Someone comes creepin' in 'ere spyin' on me just as I'm goin' into trance – the one bloody thing you know I can't abide. Could've finished me, with my groggy 'eart, it could. It's a fine bleedin' state of affairs when an honest medium can't trust 'is sitters to stay behind a curtain for ten minutes!'

'Mind your language, Brand. Ladies present,' Nye reminded him.

'William, I'd be uncommonly obliged if you would take a candle down to the cellar and switch off the electricity,' said Probert, with the authentic voice of authority.

Nye practically saluted before departing on his mission.

'Mr Brand, we *all* remained behind the curtain, I assure you,' said Alice. 'Nobody left the room.'

'Look, I don't imagine these things,' said Brand.

'My dear, nobody would suggest that you do,' said Miss Crush. 'We all heard the footsteps. You were not alone in here – there is no doubt of that. But does it not occur to you that your intruder might not have been one of us?'

'Servants, d'you mean?'

'All out. Won't be back before eleven,' said Probert. 'And if you're thinking that it might have been my wife, I'd advise you to forget it. She's so damned superstitious that she won't put her head round the door of her room until you're out of the house.'

'So it *must* have been a spirit visitor,' deduced Miss Crush.

82

'It's never 'appened like that before,' said Brand, sceptic-ally. 'The footsteps was behind me as I sat in the chair. Someone come in through the door and 'alf crossed the room, I swear it. Then 'e must've gone out again.'

Miss Crush appealed to Brand with open hands. 'Don't you understand? You have just given us a classic account of a haunting. It was a phantom that we all heard.'

Brand looked slightly mollified. 'You really think so?'

'No other explanation,' confirmed Probert.

'Well, in that case, seein' as you can't all be deceiving me,' said Brand, his speech rapidly re-acquiring its veneer of sophistication, 'I'll be content to draw a veil over the whole episode.'

'Most decent of you,' said Probert. 'As that's settled, shall we resume the equipment? Ah, William,' he said, seeing Nye reappear panting from his visit to the cellar, 'we're about to re-commence. Trot downstairs and switch it on again, will you? There's a good fellow. Perhaps you'll be so decent as to stand by the galvanometer and give us a reading, Jowett. We shall want to make sure we have a contact.'

It was the work of a few minutes to re-establish the experiment as it had been before the interruption and close the curtain. The sitters reassembled by firelight in the library, Strathmore kneeling at Jowett's side, pencil poised over pocket-book; Miss Crush with hands on the table and eyes rotated upwards to the ceiling; Probert leaning back in his chair with arms folded, watching the curtain; Nye, still recovering his breath, ogling Alice, who sat reflectively twisting her engagement ring.

'Twenty minutes to eleven,' said Strathmore.

'A reading of 202,' responded Jowett.

Somewhere outside, and from a level well below them, a ship's horn sounded a dismal note across the Thames.

'Fog, would you say?' said Nye.

Nobody seemed interested.

The fire had subsided in the grate and glowed evenly, with the occasional flare from a tiny pocket of gas that had somehow remained latent in the wood until now, and sprouted flames incredibly pure and brilliant in colour.

Miss Crush was not the first this time to detect a presence.

'Something is there,' whispered Alice Probert. 'Listen.'

'201,' said Jowett, thinking of Scotland Yard.

'Hush!'

A floorboard crunched.

'The door!' said Nye, saucer-eyed. 'The handle is turning.'

Everyone looked at the library door. He was not mistaken. The handle was turning, evenly and with a calculated pressure that made Jowett's blood run cold. When it reached the limit of its rotation the door itself swung slowly inwards. A figure took a single step into the room, and stopped. It was tall, lean in stature and sharp of feature. It was wearing a bowler hat.

'Sergeant Cribb! How the devil do you account for this?' ejaculated Jowett.

Before Cribb could respond, Strathmore barked at Jowett, 'Look to the galvanometer! The current is broken.'

'Small wonder in this blasted bear-garden!' said Probert. 'When I asked you here, Jowett, I didn't expect you to bring the rest of Scotland Yard with you. Kindly light a candle, William, and bring it to the curtain. I think we can safely assume Mr Brand won't have anything more to do with our researches after this!'

The assumption was accurate. Horrifyingly so.

When Probert tugged aside the curtain the candlelight revealed the medium supported by the chair but no longer seated in it. He was propped like a piece of timber against the angle of the left arm and back, his legs jutting stiffly to the right. His trunk was rigid, his face twisted sideways, the features contorted, with teeth bared and clenched.

'His hair!' cried Alice Probert. 'It is standing on end!'

'Keep back!' her father warned. 'Don't touch him! Downstairs, William, and switch off the current. Hurry, man, for God's sake! Strathmore, bring another candle, will you?'

'What has happened?' gasped Miss Crush.

'Electric shock, ma'am. Get back to the other room. You can't help. This is a doctor's work.'

'I must!' Miss Crush screamed hysterically, starting towards the chair.

'Hold her back!' ordered Probert.

Cribb, being nearest, reacted with commendable sharpness considering the bewildering sequence of events since he had opened the door of the room. He caught Miss Crush round the waist and tugged her towards him. She fainted in his arms.

'Typical of the woman,' said Probert. 'Take charge of her, Alice.'

Captain Nye's voice penetrated faintly from the basement. 'Electricity off, Dr Probert.'

The cutting of the current produced no appreciable change in the appearance of Brand. Dr Probert felt his pulse and put his ear to his heart. 'Gentlemen, I must try resuscitation. See if you can lift the patient on to the table in the other room, will you? Can you manage it? Where's the other man, the police sergeant?'

Nobody answered, because nobody had noticed Cribb's quick exit to the corridor, after consigning Miss Crush to an armchair and Alice Probert's smelling-salts. The sergeant's sleuthing instinct could not be deflected. He had entered the house in pursuit of a quarry, and when a loose floorboard creaked overhead, he heard it, for all the commotion over Brand.

He mounted the stairs lightly, but two at a time, and reached the first-floor landing, where five closed doors confronted him. Giving chase in a large house such as this was the very devil; he would rather track a man through the streets any day. These would be bedrooms, each with several possible hiding-places – bed, wardrobe, closet and possibly balcony. If he committed himself to a thorough search of one, he was giving his man the chance to slip out of another, down the stairs and away into the night. Lying in wait at the head of the staircase was just as futile. Any housebreaker worthy of his jemmy would resort to the drainpipes in an emergency.

Was this man a professional, though? Cribb doubted it. All the evidence so far pointed to a novice, and an incompetent one at that. In the circumstances it was not too much to hope that he might be susceptible to panic.

With one hand on the nearest door-knob, Cribb turned and unselfconsciously addressed the empty landing. 'Very well, you men. I want a thorough search made of every room. Sergeant, take two men and start with that one. I shall be looking in here. Brown, go down for reinforcements, will you? We need half a dozen able-bodied men. At the double. Avoid violence if possible, everyone. The suspect may be ready to give himself up.' Putting his hand over his mouth, he added in two well disguised and distinctively different voices, 'Very good, sir.' 'Right, sir.' He opened the door and slammed it shut immediately. Then he crossed the landing, treading heavily, opened the nearest door and stepped inside, leaving it ajar, to wait developments.

It was unfortunate after a dramatic cameo of such quality and ingenuity that he chose the room he did, for immediately on entering it he was felled by a crack on the head that would probably have brained him but for his bowler. He hit the floor in company with the shattered fragments of a water-jug and lay momentarily unable to move as his assailant stumbled over him and across the landing to the second-floor stairs.

By a stupendous effort of will Cribb engineered himself from the horizontal to the vertical and lurched outside, in time to meet Inspector Jowett, attracted upstairs by the voices.

'Good God, Cribb! What are you doing *now*?'

'Pur – pursuing a suspect, sir.'

'Which way did he go?'

'Upstairs, sir,' gasped Cribb.

Jowett put up his right arm, as if directing traffic. 'Get after him, then. No time to lose.'

'I might need help, sir.'

'I'll be the judge of that, Sergeant. I won't be far behind you, depend upon it.'

It occurred to Cribb as he hobbled upstairs, supporting himself on the banister, that his impersonation of an inspector deploying personnel had lacked the spark of realism. Jowett did it much more convincingly.

He was halfway upstairs when he remembered Mrs Probert. It was all very well running your quarry to earth at the top of a house, but what if he chose to make his final stand in a room already occupied by a woman in fear of her life?

She would scream.

She did. It was powerful enough to rattle the stair-rods. She was still screaming when Cribb reached her. Insensible at her feet lay Professor Eustace Quayle. Beside him was the volume of *Notable British Sermons* Mrs Probert had hurled at his head.

7

'Pause and collect yourself! We understand!
That's the bad memory, or the natural shock,
Or the unexplained *phenomena*!'

'He has gone, I'm afraid,' said Dr Probert, refastening his shirtsleeves. Half an hour's concentrated attempt to resuscitate Peter Brand had produced not a glimmer of life. The body lay as it had first been put down on the table in the library. The rest of Dr Probert's guests and family stood in attendance.

'Passed over?' queried Miss Crush, unable, apparently, to accept the information.

'Joined the majority, madam,' said Strathmore, in language she would understand.

'Support her, Alice!' ordered Probert. 'She's going again.'

'How the deuce does a thing like this happen?' asked Nye, ignoring the attempt to stop Miss Crush from hitting the floor.

'That will be for a coroner to decide,' said Probert. 'I suspect that the immediate cause of death is heart failure induced by an electric shock. The muscular contraction and the peculiar behaviour of the hair suggests nothing else to me. A man with a heart condition such as his would be vulnerable to a severe electric shock.'

'But you led us to believe that the apparatus was entirely safe,' said Nye. 'How could he have received a severe shock?'

Probert shook his head. 'William, I am at a loss to account for it. Everything will have to be examined by experts.'

'That's a fact, sir,' said Cribb, speaking from the study. 'We shall have to arrange for this room to be locked until it's been seen. I've got a shrewd idea that unless you take precautions the housemaid will be here at some ungodly hour tomorrow morning pushing a carpet-sweeper through the wires.'

'You may have the key for as long as you need it,' said Probert, much subdued in manner.

'I'll take charge of it,' said Jowett, leaving no doubt who was the senior officer present. 'This is the moment I think, when I should explain to your guests, Probert, that I am a detective-inspector. My connection with Great Scotland Yard you have already disclosed, notwithstanding my request to the contrary. The man who interrupted the seance is Detective-Sergeant Cribb, and his arrival on the scene was as surprising to me as it was to the rest of you. We now know that he was pursuing a man who had illegally entered this house, the person known as Professor Quayle. Where have you put Quayle for the present, Cribb?'

'The kitchen, sir. Handcuffed him to the range. He'll keep nice and warm until we're ready for him.' Cribb smiled at Mrs Probert, who had come downstairs and was sitting inconspicuously between two bookcases. 'That was a neat a knockdown as I've seen, ma'am, if you'll allow me to say so.'

'It was pure fright,' said Mrs Probert simply. 'I heard the voices on the landing underneath me and I came to the conclusion that an army was on its way up to my room. Waiting for them to burst in on me was too much to endure, so I stood at my door with the first thing that came to hand, the book I was reading. I thought it would show that I was not prepared to submit without a fight. I had a knitting-needle ready for the next man. It was a good thing you stopped the other side of Professor Quayle, Sergeant.'

'I think we should not concern ourselves too much with Quayle at this juncture,' said Jowett firmly. 'It seems evident that by coincidence two lamentable events occurred in this house tonight within minutes of each other. Speaking as the senior police officer present, I must insist that the sudden death of Mr Brand has priority in our investigations. Can't you cover him over, or something, Probert? The sight of him is obviously distressing the ladies.'

'I'll fetch a sheet,' said Mrs Probert, going to the door.

'A coincidence, you say,' said Strathmore. 'I'm doubtful of that, Inspector.'

Jowett crossed his arms challengingly. 'Exactly what do you intend by that remark, sir?'

'Why, that it seems reasonable to suppose that Brand's accident and Quayle's presence here are not unconnected. The men are professional collaborators, are they not?'

'They *were*,' said Probert.

'And they lodged in the same house,' continued Strathmore. 'As an investigator of the occult, I am bound to reflect on what has happened this evening and ask myself whether Quayle was here in the role of accomplice, to assist the medium in producing fraudulent phenomena. It is nothing unusual in the annals of spiritualism, I assure you.'

'That's a quick turn round,' said Nye. 'An hour ago you were ready to tell the world that eternal life was an established fact.'

'And what grounds do you have for suggesting this was a fraudulent seance?' demanded Miss Crush, now fully conscious, and brandishing the smelling-salts at Strathmore. 'The things I heard and saw tonight were genuine, I am perfectly confident. You all experienced them – the rappings, the spirit hand and the oranges being thrown about and the vase overturned while we all had our hands linked. If you are suggesting Professor Quayle was in the room with us throwing fruit in our faces I think you have a lot of explaining to do. Do you suppose he was under the table as well, tugging at our clothes? Alice, you felt the hand touching you, didn't you?'

'Yes, I did, most certainly. It touched the hem of my dress and pulled it several times. And in the second seance, my hair was stroked. I told you all at the time. You could *see* that nobody was in the room but ourselves.' Alice Probert's eyes shone with earnestness. She spoke with all the passion of her nineteen years, her forehead creasing prettily with the importance of it all.

'Delusions, indubitably,' said Strathmore. 'You were predisposed to expect something of the sort.' He chuckled deep in his throat. 'This isn't the first time I've heard one of the fair sex claim that somebody touched her in the dark, my dear.'

She returned a withering look. 'That is an observation that reflects only upon you, Mr Strathmore.'

'Careful how you speak to my fiancée, sir,' warned Nye, with as much effect as a man who puts *Beware of the Dog* on his gate after his pet has savaged the neighbour.

Probert had a constructive suggestion to make. 'We might establish whether Brand was fraudulent by turning out his pockets. They will need to be emptied for identification purposes. If there's a white glove in there, or a hand made of plaster of Paris, we shall know Strathmore's suspicions are correct. What do you say, Inspector.'

'I have no objection,' answered Jowett, pleased to be consulted. It had begun to look as if he was losing control of the discussion. He took a step towards the body, checked and on second thoughts delegated the duty to Cribb. 'Sergeant, come over here and go through the pockets, will you? I shall make an inventory as you do so.'

Cribb stepped briskly forward. 'Left hand trouser pocket, sir: nothing. Right hand: some money, two shillings and sevenpence halfpenny. Hip pocket: nothing. Jacket pocket, left hand outside: cigarette case, silver, and box of safety matches, Bryant and May. Right hand: two keys on a ring. Ticket pocket: railway ticket, third class return, Richmond to Waterloo. Breast pocket, left hand inside: nothing. Right hand: wallet, pigskin, containing two penny postage stamps, numerous betting-tickets and a photograph, somewhat dog-eared, of a lady in the – er – music-hall costume. There's numbers on the back, sir.'

'The back of the photograph, I trust,' said Jowett drily. 'Let me see.'

Cribb handed it discreetly face downwards to his superior. Jowett frowned. There were two sets of neatly-formed numbers: 469 and below it 9281, followed by a square, the same size as the figures.

'Not significant, in my opinion,' said Jowett, after a pause. He turned the photograph over, blushed, and handed it back to Cribb. 'Carry on, Sergeant.'

'Top pocket: nothing, sir. Waistcoat, left hand side: nothing. Right hand: silver watch and chain, inscribed "P. B." That's all, sir.'

Cribb put the objects in a neat arrangement on the table at the dead man's feet. Mrs Probert came forward with a sheet and draped it over the body.

'That seems to answer your point, Mr Strathmore,' said Jowett. 'There's nothing here to suggest he was a fraud.'

'I hope certain people feel suitably ashamed of themselves,' said Miss Crush in a stage whisper.

'Very well, the medium had no evidence of trickery on his person,' Strathmore conceded. 'That is not to have prevented him from passing things to his collaborator. I suggest we make a similar search of Quayle.'

'Done, sir,' said Cribb. 'He's carrying a railway ticket, twelve and sixpence and a hip-flask of gin, which fortunately survived his fall.'

Jowett gave the sort of cough a chairman gives to call a meeting to order. 'Ladies and gentlemen, I think we have explored this avenue of inquiry for long enough. It has produced nothing of consequence. I propose that we now confine ourselves strictly to the circumstances of Mr Brand's unfortunate demise. Do I understand that you have something to contribute, madam?' He peered warily at Miss Crush, who had been waving her hand throughout his speech.

'Yes,' she said. 'Shouldn't somebody go and fetch a policeman?'

94

Even in the presence of death, unforced laughter is difficult to suppress. It took several seconds for Jowett to restore order. 'I believe, madam, that you were insensible when I introduced myself just now. I am Detective-Inspector Jowett of the Criminal Investigation Department, Great Scotland Yard, and I will suffice for a policeman. My assistant here is Sergeant Cribb, whom I was led to believe has already interviewed you at your house. He is a policeman, too.'

'I should have remembered,' said Miss Crush, flapping her hand at the inspector. 'I think of him as a sensitive, you see, not an officer of the law. It would help if you both wore uniforms.' She sighed and looked misty-eyed. 'I think tall helmets are very *chic*.'

Jowett closed his eyes, and said with deliberation, 'I need to determine the circumstances leading to Mr Brand's decease. I shall require a statement from each of you, but before we begin the formalities, is there anyone with anything to say bearing on the accident which has not been mentioned already?'

'I think so, sir,' said Cribb. 'If you'll step into the study, I can show you.' He crossed the room with Jowett following and crouched in front of the chair in which Brand had died. 'Put your hand on the carpet here, sir. Feel it? It's damp over quite a large patch eighteen inches in front of the chair. When we found the body the feet were positioned on this patch. I don't regard myself as much of a scientist, but I know that water can conduct electricity, and that electricity tends to go to earth. If Mr Brand started with his feet under the chair on this dry area, but moved them forward during the experiment, mightn't it have diverted the path of the current so that it flowed through the length of his body to earth? I think it's pertinent to ask how the wet patch got here.'

'That's no mystery,' said Probert at once. 'I kicked over a bowl of salt solution we used to make a good contact for the terminals.'

'When did this happen, sir?'

'Halfway through, when Brand called me from behind the curtain. We were totally in darkness, if you follow me, and I blundered into the thing. It made no difference, though. He didn't get a shock, or anything.'

'Probably not, sir, if his feet were on the dry part of the carpet. He'd get his shock when he moved them forward.'

'I see your point, Sergeant, but it still doesn't explain how the shock could have killed him. The current couldn't change, you see. It was no more than a trickle. Several of us tried it.'

'Couldn't feel a thing,' Nye confessed.

'The transformer was the safeguard, you understand,' continued Probert. 'It reduced the electromotive force to twenty volts, and that won't kill a man, I assure you.'

Cribb looked thoughtfully at the wooden box from which the wires trailed. 'This cable connected to the other side of the transformer leads up from the batteries in the cellar, does it, sir?'

'Yes, that's the main lead. It carries 416 volts. If I'd connected *that* to the chair it would have been lethal.'

'And if there was a fault in the transformer?'

Probert shook his head emphatically. 'I'm damned sure there wasn't, Sergeant. Have it checked, by all means, but you'll find it's working perfectly. Otherwise we shouldn't have got the galvanometer readings we did.

Heavens, at 416 volts the blasted galvanometer would have been burnt out!'

Cribb stood up and massaged the side of his face, a tactful way of indicating to Jowett that he was at liberty to take over the questioning if he wished. There was silence except for the rasp of Cribb's side-whiskers, so he began again. 'Dr Probert, you mentioned that Brand called out to you, and that was how you came to overturn the bowl of water. What did he want?'

'He claimed that somebody had come into the study while he was in trance. He was most indignant about it, and only calmed down when we suggested it must have been a spirit. All the people in the house except my wife were present in the library, you see.'

'That was what you supposed at the time, sir.'

'Good God, I'd forgotten! It could have been Quayle who interrupted him – or even you!'

'Not me, sir, I assure you, but Professor Quayle is a possibility. Quite an engaging one. I followed him into the house through the back door. You ought to have a word with your servants about that, sir. We spend a lot of time in the Force reminding people about doors they haven't locked. Anyway, I think the professor must have heard me in pursuit, because he was nowhere to be seen by the time I got up here from the basement. It's my guess now that he let himself in through the study door to give me the slip. He probably couldn't see a thing when he first came in.'

'Of course!' said Nye excitedly. 'The silly blighter cracked his foot against the transformer and shot 400 volts into Brand, poor beggar.'

'Impossible!' said Probert with a glare. 'Brand was perfectly all right when we pulled aside the curtain. The accident happened later, between the time when we withdrew and closed the curtain for the second time and when the Sergeant came in through the library door. At that time Quayle was definitely not in the study.'

'He'd given me the slip, sir,' said Cribb. 'The next I heard from him was the creaking of a floorboard upstairs after we discovered what had happened in here. He couldn't get out through the basement because Captain Nye was down there switching off the current, so he went upstairs instead.'

'As we discovered,' said Probert.

'As I did,' his wife corrected him.

'What nobody has made clear,' said Alice, 'is why Professor Quayle came into the house at all. If it wasn't to assist Mr Brand, as now seems clear, what *was* the purpose of his presence here?'

Cribb shot an inquiring glance at his superior. 'I was rather hoping to extract that information from the professor himself, miss. If Inspector Jowett was proposing to collect statements from you all, I wondered if I might be spared to put some questions across the kitchen table downstairs. Only, of course, if you were planning things that way, sir.'

Jowett nodded, the first positive thing he had achieved in ten minutes. 'That was precisely what I was coming to, Sergeant.'

'Thank you, sir. It looks like being a long night, so while I'm down there, I'll put the kettle on, if I may. I'll stand it on the range beside the professor and see which one sings first.'

As it turned out, the interview could not take place in the kitchen. Hitchman, the Proberts' deaf maidservant, had returned from her evening off and was threatening the professor with a meat-hook when Cribb got down there. The kitchen was her domain and she was clearly quite intractable, so he side-stepped her, unlocked the professor, marched him upstairs and obtained the key to the picture-gallery from Probert.

'Sit down, sir,' he said, poking the professor in the chest with sufficient firmness to park him in the flirtation settee. 'I shan't join you. Nothing personal intended, but I like to see a man's eyes when I ask him questions. In case you wondered, we ain't here to look at the ladies on the wall, and I don't propose to compete with 'em.' He pulled the draw-string at the side of one of Dr Probert's naked goddesses, who was partially in view, then smartly turned about, pointed a finger at Quayle and asked, 'What have you done with the Etty?'

'The what?' asked Quayle, in a voice so thin nobody would have believe it had harangued an audience from the platform of the Store Street Hall.

'*Sleeping Nymph and Satyrs.* Occupied a place on the wall behind you until last Friday week. Dr Probert wants it back. I hope it ain't mutilated.'

'I don't know anything about this, Constable.'

'Sergeant, if you please. Cribb's the name. Don't waste my time. I want some sleep tonight. Etty was the artist, you see.'

'I don't think I've heard of him.'

'That's evident,' said Cribb, 'or you wouldn't have walked out with the canvas you did. There's better things on these walls than Ettys, I can tell you. You and I might say there isn't much to choose between buxom wenches in the buff, but we'd be wrong. There's some here worth ten of your Ettys. French ones. No man of culture would have helped himself to an English nymph when there was mademoiselles to be had. And why take only one, when you could have had an armful? You can't even cut a canvas neatly off its frame. You're a raw beginner, Professor, no doubt of it.'

Quayle said nothing, but his tongue raced nervously round his lips, moistening them.

'It was the same at Miss Crush's,' Cribb went on. 'You took a piece of common Royal Worcester when you could have had a priceless Minton. It was plain to me that you knew as much about china as you did about nudes, or house-breaking. You made a shocking mess of Dr Probert's pantry, climbing in through all the biscuits and pearl barley, didn't you? So it didn't take a Scotland Yard man to work out that the thief wasn't a professional cracksman.

'How did I come to suspect you? Well, at first I did what you intended – I suspected Peter Brand instead. It was obvious the thief was primed. He knew the only favourable times to rob the houses: when the owners were out visiting. Consider the sequence of events. On October 15th there's a seance at Miss Crush's at which Brand and Dr Probert are guests. The doctor very civilly invites Miss Crush back to his house for a return seance on October 31st. She attends, and so does Brand. During the evening Dr Probert makes reference to a lecture he is going to give, which his wife and daughter will attend. The seance comes to an end, Brand leaves, and an hour later so does Miss Crush. When she gets home she discovers the theft of her vase. On November 6th, the night of the lecture, the Proberts' house is broken into, and a picture stolen. Who can I suspect but Brand, the only person other than the doctor and Miss

Crush who was present at both seances and knew when to execute the burglaries?'

'It seems a reasonable inference to make,' said Quayle guardedly. 'He is of humble extraction, as you must have gathered from his occasional lapses of speech. His father was a common cabman, I believe. A person of that class admitted suddenly to the residences of the well-to-do is subject to certain temptations, is he not?'

'Ah,' said Cribb, putting up a forefinger. 'That's what you wanted me to think, and so I did for a short time. Until I clapped my eyes on you, Professor.'

'Where was this?'

'Don't look so alarmed. It wasn't in Probert's garden. It was legitimate enough at the time – your lantern lecture at the Store Street Hall.'

'You were there?'

'My assistant is Constable Thackeray, the man with the handcuffs.'

'I might have guessed.'

'You might, sir. You looked a trifle worried when Peter Brand removed the handcuffs from the envelope, as I recall, but so did Brand, of course. I must be fair. Before that, though, I was already starting to turn things over in my mind. It seemed to me that Peter Brand was a young man with ambition. He was earning something of a reputation in the metropolis. What was it? Spirit-writing in Camberwell and the levitation of the suite of furniture in Hampstead? At any rate, there can't be many mediums of twenty capable of sharing the bill with you at the Store Street Hall.'

'It was only at my invitation,' insisted Quayle.

'The whole point is,' Cribb continued, 'that he was

starting to earn fat fees, and the prospects were even better. Why should he queer his own pitch by robbing the clients when he was fleecing them handsomely already? It made no sense.'

'Fleecing them?' repeated Quayle. 'What do you mean by that?'

'Simply that I class young Brand with any other sharp, and it's my experience that the needle-pointed fraternity don't play two games at once.'

'I hope you are not equating spiritualism with race-course practices.'

'It's all a way of lining your pocket, as I see it,' said Cribb. 'You don't find your thimble-rigger picking pockets at the same time as he works the cups. When young Brand picked the handcuffs out of the envelope at the meeting, he was terrified, I could see that. But it wasn't on account of the Etty or the Worcester vase; it was because he was afraid we'd tumbled to the fact that he already knew Miss Crush and all about her Uncle Walter.'

'Oh that,' said Quayle dismissively. 'Pure opportunism. It was perfectly legitimate.'

'I'd like to hear you justify that to your audience,' said Cribb. 'However, Brand, for whatever reason, took the first opportunity of dashing for the exit. We caught up with him a few yards short of Tottenham Court Road. Do you know, Professor, he didn't even know the vase had gone from Miss Crush's house, and when I mentioned it, he thought it was the Minton that must have been taken. Unlike you, you see, he can tell the value of a piece of china. He also talked about you.'

Quayle's eyes flashed with fury. 'Did he? The little guttersnipe!'

'Yes. Called you a regular pal, if I recall correctly. Said that you took him in and taught him the rudiments of table-tapping.'

'Oh, did he?' Quayle rapidly switched to a conciliatory tone. 'That's perfectly true, of course. I gave him introductions to some of the best addresses in London.'

'So I heard,' said Cribb. 'Just when you were slipping out of public favour, too. It takes a generous-hearted man to lend a helping hand to an up-and-coming youngster at a time like that.'

'I'm glad you appreciate the fact.'

'I asked myself why you did it.'

'From altruism, Sergeant.'

Cribb walked to the sideboard and poured a glass of water from the flask there. 'You've got all the answers ready, haven't you? No, a man in your shoes doesn't hand his livelihood over to an upstart for no good reason. I know why you did it. You gave him the helping hand to let him get ahead of you so that you could stab him in the back. Figuratively speaking, of course.'

Quayle shook his head so vigorously that his cheeks quivered. 'Arrant nonsense!'

'In that way there was far more chance of winning back the favour of your patrons. Have you ever studied prize-fighting? You've got a lot in common with the great Jem Mace. Do you know, Professor, there's only one thing that the Fancy like better than a novice who comes fresh to win a championship, and that's the old'un who comes back to knock him out. It's a sound principle, and it would have worked for you if you hadn't been such a poor hand as a thief. All the conditions were right. Brand didn't have the slightest notion of what you were planning, so he fed you all the information you needed. You broke into the houses when everyone was out and found the things of value without trouble. Unhappily, that's where your plan ran into difficulties, because you picked the wrong things to steal. The objects didn't matter to you; it was the act of theft that was important. That was all that was necessary to scotch Peter Brand's career. Far better to do it that way, you decided, than expose him as a fraudulent medium, which would have raised doubts about mediums in general.'

'This is all very ingenious, Sergeant, but where is it leading us?' said Quayle in a bored voice. 'You can prove nothing except that I was in this house tonight. My presence here is quite contrary to your theories, in fact.'

'It is indeed, sir. I fully expected you to break into the empty residence of one of the guests. I've got Constable Thackeray on duty at this moment at Miss Crush's place.'

'Really? How ridiculous!'

'Yes, I didn't expect you here tonight, but since you came, I felt obliged to follow you. And now I am arresting you on suspicion of entering this dwelling-house tonight with intent to commit a felony. That's just a start, sir. I expect to bring several charges later, including the theft on November 6th of one picture entitled *Sleeping Nymph and Satyrs*, the property of Dr Probert.'

'I deny it! You have no proof.'

'But I have,' said Cribb. 'It's in this glass of water.' He held the still half-full tumbler six inches in front of the professor's eyes. 'See the small white object lying on the bottom? I put it in the glass a few minutes ago. It's swelling nicely, ain't it? I removed several like it from your trouser turn-ups when we carried you downstairs after Mrs Probert knocked you senseless with her book.'

'What is it, for God's sake?'

'I don't go in for stews over-much, sir, but I think I know what this is. There's a lot of 'em lying where you knocked 'em over climbing in through Dr Probert's pantry. Devilish little things. Pearl barley, Professor, pearl barley.'

8

Here's a choice birth o' the supernatural . . .

A hacking cough shattered the silence. 'Lord help us!' said Constable Thackeray to himself.

He should have been in bed. Eleven hours he had squatted behind a tree opposite Miss Crush's house in Eaton Square. Eleven hours on one of the bleakest nights in November. By dawn he could have passed for Uncle Walter, he was so blanched by frost. And what had it achieved, apart from the likely onset of chronic pneumonia?

Nothing.

Not a living soul has approached the terrace until eight in the morning, when Cribb appeared and gave the sort of whistle a dog-owner gives when his animal lingers too long in the bushes. 'I've got a job for you, Thackeray,' he said, as if eleven hours behind a tree had not been employment at all. 'Cut along to Sloane Square and take the Metropolitan line to Praed Street. It's a short step from there to Homer Court. Here's the key to number 10, Professor Quayle's house. Let yourself in and locate Dr Probert's missing picture in the umbrella stand. Miss Crush's vase should be in a cabinet in the bathroom. No need to look surprised, Constable. Quayle confessed to me six hours ago. Oh, and make a list of Peter Brand's personal effects, will you? He won't be in his rooms. Died in mysterious circumstances last night. Lord, yes, I've been busy since I last saw you. I'm off to get some sleep now. Report to me at two o'clock, will you? Sharp, mind.'

As usual, there was no answering Cribb. He climbed back into a waiting cab before Thackeray had a chance to put two words together. All a man could do in the circumstances was brush off the worst of the frost and hobble away to the station, trying not to mind the chilblains.

Cribb had not mentioned it, but Thackeray decided to assume his order included a short stop at the soup-stall in Sloane Square for a bowl of ox-tail. He would make sure the twopence went into his diary as legitimate expenses, too, and if he had to buy wintergreen ointment for his toes he was going to put that down as well, whatever anyone said.

Quayle's house was large and detached, not so fashionably situated as Miss Crush's, but certainly no slum. Remarkable that an occupation concerned with spiritual things should be so productive of worldly comforts. Thackeray had let himself in, removed the rolled-up Etty from a collection of walking-sticks and umbrellas and carried it upstairs to the second floor, collecting the Royal Worcester from the bathroom on the way. Both now lay on the floor of Peter Brand's sitting-room, the painting still unfurled. There was not the slightest doubt that it was Dr Probert's nymph. Cribb was sickeningly unlikely to have made a mistake. And Thackeray with his chilblains felt no overmastering urge to gaze at a naked form of either sex.

It was a salutary experience to occupy a dead man's room and see the evidence of recent occupation, a discarded

107

shirt over a chair-back, the collar on the floor, orange-peel in the grate and unwashed plates on the table. That it was a bachelor establishment was clear from the reek of stale tobacco. The picture over the mantelpiece was of a race-horse and there were betting-tickets strewn about the floor.

Thackeray had withdrawn his notebook and was starting to record the contents of the room when his work was interrupted by a clatter at the front door downstairs. He went to the window and peered out. A cab was drawn up outside. Uncertain what to expect, he descended the two flights of stairs and opened the door.

A cabman was standing in the porch, a barrel-shaped man in a brown bowler and one of those enormous great-coats that reached from chin to bootlaces, the hallmark of the trade. The number 469 was prominently displayed on his badge. What was visible of his hair was grey, and his moustache protruded over his lips and was damp at the extremities.

He touched his hat. 'Morning, sir. I've come for Mr Brand's things.'

'His things?' repeated Thackeray.

''E's dead, ain't 'e? Won't be wanting 'em now.'

'How do you know he's dead?'

The cabby shrugged his shoulders. 'Common knowledge by now. News travels fast in my occupation. I 'eard about it at the cab shelter by Paddington station. 'Ad a fatal accident in Richmond, didn't 'e? Who are you, if you ain't the undertaker?'

'I was about to ask the same question,' said Thackeray.

'Charlie Brand, sir. Father of the deceased.'

'I see. I'm sorry.'

'No need to be. 'E wasn't much to me.'

'Is that so? I'm a police officer. Detective-Constable Thackeray. Plain clothes duty.'

'What you doing 'ere, then? Picking up a fresh set of plain clothes?'

'Certainly not,' said Thackeray with dignity. 'I'm here to make a list of the deceased's possessions.'

'And I'm 'ere to collect 'em,' said the cabman. 'Next of kin, you see. Prior claim. I think I 'ave the right to look over that list of yours. There should be a silver watch somewhere. It wouldn't be in your pocket by any chance, would it?'

'It would not,' said Thackeray firmly. 'I have a watch of my own with my personal number scratched on the back. If you want to come inside you'd better keep a civil tongue in your head, cabman. How am I to know you're Brand's father, anyway?'

The cabman tapped his badge. 'This is *my* personal number, and you can check it in the 'Ackney Carriage Licensing Department, right under your police office in Great Scotland Yard. Brand, Charles Edgar, on the box for forty-six years, excepting three in the Crimea. When I started, there wasn't no detectives to speak of. The thief-takers was the Runners, and a fine body of men they was.' He peered closely at Thackeray. 'I suppose you wasn't one, by any chance?'

'Lord, no!' said Thackeray. 'I was just a babe in arms in them days. You'd better come in, then, Mr Brand. I can't allow you to cart anything away, but I suppose I ought to let you see what's there.'

'Rubbish mostly, if you ask me,' Brand senior remarked, as he followed Thackeray upstairs. On the first-floor landing he paused to gather breath for the second flight. 'You 'aven't come across the watch, then?'

109

Thackeray turned. 'I have not, cabman, and I swear I'll lay one on you if I hear another word about it.'

In Brand's room they paused just outside the door. The cabman had not endeared himself much to Thackeray so far, but he was entitled to respect that is due to any bereaved parent. It was impossible not to respond to the numerous reminders in the room of the life so suddenly cut short.

The response, in Brand senior's case, was unsentimental: 'I suppose the picture might raise a pound or two, but I don't see much else 'ere. You don't suppose the landlord's been round already and 'ad the pick of the stuff, do you?'

'Impossible,' said Thackeray. 'The landlord's been in custody all night.'

'Copped 'im, 'ave you? What was 'e doing – keeping a disorderly 'ouse?'

'That's no concern of yours, cabman,' Thackeray retorted. 'If you're quite sure there's nothing here worth having, don't let me delay you any longer. I've got my work to do.'

Brand Senior seemed to interpret this as an invitation to stay and watch. He lowered himself into an arm-chair, took out a pipe, filled it, thrust it between his moustache and his muffler, lighted it and was temporarily lost to view in the resulting smoke. 'This don't surprise me in the least,' he said, clearing a shaft in the cloud with his hand. 'The boy's been keeping bad company for years. It wasn't the way 'e was brought up, I can tell you. 'E was reared with the end of my belt, was that boy. I was mother and father to 'im for ten years – ten years, Officer. Taught 'im the Ten Commandments and 'is numbers and 'ow to groom the 'orse and look what 'e came to! I might as well 'ave saved meself the exercise.'

'Did his mother die young?' inquired Thackeray, trying

110

to dredge up a scrap of sympathy for this peculiarly unsympathetic old man.

'Still alive, so far as I know,' said Brand unhelpfully.

'You parted company, then?'

'Company?' Brand laughed with such an eruption that it brought on a fit of coughing. 'It never got as far as company. Blimey no, it was nothing like that.' He produced a large red handkerchief and dried the corners of his eyes. 'Now we've started, I'd better tell you all about it, or you'll go on asking your cock-eyed questions till it's time for me to go. Did you see my 'orse as you opened the front door just now?'

'I can't say I noticed him particularly,' admitted Thackeray, uncertain what the horse had to do with the story.

'That's my fourth out there,' continued Brand Senior. 'Nine-year-old gelding, and a very fine shape for a cabber, too. Twenty year ago the beast between them shafts was a bag o' bones, Officer, I don't mind admitting it. I called 'im Ezekiel, after the prophet what told the story of the bones that came to life. If you'd seen my Ezekiel standing in the cab-rank in The Strand you'd say 'e was the living proof of that story. You might think 'e got like that from poor feeding, and I suppose there's a grain of truth in that, because I was up against 'ard times in them days, but I'm inclined to think 'e was sparely built, same as certain 'umans are. Ezekiel just *looked* pathetic, but 'e was given the nose-bag as often as any other animal on the rank.'

'Get to the point, for God's sake, cabman,' requested Thackeray. 'I didn't get any sleep last night.'

'All right. 'Old on, mate. Now one spring morning I'm waiting in the rank as usual when a flunkey of some sort comes walking along the pavement sizing us up, like. 'E takes a long look at Ezekiel and after a bit 'e comes up to me and says, "You'll do. I'm 'iring you for the hour." Now if there's one thing certain to start a riot in the cab-rank it's jumping the line, so I tells the flunkey 'e must go to the front and take the first cab in the rank. "Not on your life," says 'e. "I want you, and if I 'ave to wait 'alf an hour for you that's all the same to me." Sure enough 'e waits for twenty minutes, till it's my turn at the front, then 'e climbs aboard, giving me an address in Russell Square. "That won't take an hour," says I. "Never you mind," says 'e. So I cracks me whip and old Ezekiel gets us there inside ten minutes. "Wait 'ere, cabby," says the flunkey, and disappears inside a big 'ouse. Presently out 'e comes with a young lady, got up to the nines. A stunner she was, I promise you. 'E 'ands 'er into the cab and tells me to take 'er round Regent's Park, driving slow. Now I don't 'ave to tell you that it weren't the thing at all in them days any more than it is now for a single woman to drive alone in a four-wheeler.'

'Not a respectable woman,' said Thackeray.

'That's my point,' said Brand, blowing another cloud of smoke in Thackeray's direction. 'I could see she was well turned-out, but so was Skittles – remember 'er, Officer? – and 'alf-a-dozen others at that time. Mine was a respectable cab and I didn't want no part in anything irregular.'

'All right,' said Thackeray. 'You don't need to convince me. Get on with the story.'

'Well, I'm sitting on me box wondering what she's 'ired me for, when she taps on the roof with 'er parasol. I opens the 'atch and she tells me to stop the cab. "This 'orse of yours," she says, when I've pulled Ezekiel's 'ead back and stopped. "It's in a pitiful condition. I'd like to give it a carrot." "Well, Miss," says I, "if you 'ad one with you, I'd be 'appy for Ezekiel to 'ave it." "I 'ave," says she, and bless me if she don't fetch one out of 'er bag and push it through the 'atch. "Give it to 'im now," she says, "and I'll give you a shilling extra with the fare." So I obliged the lady and Ezekiel got 'is carrot. That old 'ack never 'ad a bigger surprise in all 'is life. When I'd fed 'im she said she'd like to come down and stroke 'is nose. I wasn't too 'appy about that, because Ezekiel was an evil-tempered brute at the best of times, even after 'e'd been fed, but 'appily there wasn't no incident. She climbs back into the cab and we completes the turn round the Park and back to Russell Square. "Call for me at the same time tomorrow," she says, and gives me three and six, I tell no lie.'

'Did you go?'

'Of course I did. A cabby don't say no to that sort of money. The same thing 'appened for the next five days and Ezekiel was getting quite a frisky look to 'im as we bowled into Russell Square each morning. The lady told me she belonged to some society for the welfare of cab-'orses and she'd sent 'er servant out to find the most broken-down old cabber on the rank. Then one morning she says, "Let's go up to 'Ampstead today. We can take Ezekiel up to Parliament 'Ill Fields. There's some long grass there and we'll give 'im the time of 'is life." So off we trot through Camden and Kentish Town and sure enough there's a lovely stretch of grass behind Gospel Oak station. "Ain't you going to unbridle 'im?" she asks me, when I've led 'im off the road, and I swear it now, Officer, there was a look in that young woman's eye that was beginning to unbridle *me*, never mind the 'orse. Anyway, I got 'er down from the cab and let Ezekiel out of the shafts, and we walked a little way to a quiet spot, where she suggested we sat down. We was still

113

in view of Ezekiel and the cab, but out of sight of the road, if you understand me.'

'I'm beginning to,' said Thackeray.

'After a bit she says, "Ezekiel already looks a better 'orse. You can't see 'is ribs quite so easy now, can you?" "No," says I, "you've spoilt 'im proper. I suppose you'll be looking for another starving old cabber soon." "That's my mission in life," she says. "I want to rescue all the cab-'orses I can. Yes, I think this will 'ave to be the last outing I 'ave with Ezekiel, but I want you to treat 'im proper from now on, cabman. Feed and water 'im regular, or the Society will get to 'ear of it. And don't put inferior stuff into 'is nosebag. 'Orses like oats. But you're a kind man, I can see. You'll treat Ezekiel well." And with that she leans across and plants a kiss on my cheek. Now being the way I am, Officer, I'm not one to let a chance slip by. I put my arms around the lady and returned the compliment. One thing led to another and, to phrase it delicate, Ezekiel 'ad to wait a long time for 'is oats, but I got mine that afternoon.' The cabman slowly formed another dense cloud of smoke as he recollected the occasion. 'It was the last time I was to see 'er for over a year, and being a man of honour I didn't even ask for the fare when we got back to Russell Square.'

'Very thoughtful,' said Thackeray.

'Yes, it wasn't till September that I 'eard anything of 'er, and by then Ezekiel was looking as scraggy as ever. When the flunkey found me in the cabman's shelter I thought my luck was in again. I bowled off round Russell Square and I swear old Ezekiel knew where we was 'eading for and galloped all the way.

'When we got there, out comes the lady and climbs inside without even looking at the 'orse or me and calls out an address in Notting 'Ill Gate. It don't make no sense to me, but I know my job, so away we goes. And when we get there it's a shabby little terraced 'ouse, but out she gets and asks me to come in too. A big woman comes to the door and lets us in without a word. She shows us the parlour and what do you think is there? A baby, Officer, three months old and 'owling fit to burst. "You can pick it up," says me passenger. "It's yours. I've brought it into the world and provided for it up to now, but I can't keep it. It wouldn't be possible for a woman in my position. So it's yours, cabman. Look after it won't you?" I was so surprised, Officer, that I picked it up without a word and do you know it stopped bellowing at once? "There will be money provided regular for its upkeep," she told me. "Mrs 'Awkins 'ere will take care of it by day until it's old enough to join you on the cab, but you must collect it every night. It will need to know its father. Be good enough not to get in touch with me after today. The baby's name is Peter, and you'd better treat 'im kinder than that unfortunate 'orse of yours, or Mrs 'Awkins will fetch in the law." And I could see by the way the fat woman wagged 'er 'ead at me that she didn't like the look of me at all.'

'What a facer!' said Thackeray. 'What did you do?'

'Exactly what they wanted. I took the child and brought it up, as I've told you. As soon as it was old enough I told 'Awkins 'er services wasn't required no more. Money arrived regular by way of the flunkey until the boy was ten years old and could earn for 'imself.'

'What work did you put him to?' asked Thackeray.

'Glimming, at first.'

'What's that?'

'That's 'olding cab doors open for passengers, to save the cabby from getting off 'is box. You must 'ave seen the boys along the rank stretching their arms across the cab wheels to stop the ladies' dresses from getting soiled. It's worth a copper or two most times. 'E done that for about a year, and then 'e went 'is own way. I 'ad it in mind to get 'im 'prenticed, but 'e can't read or write, you see, and there wasn't no openings. I believe 'e sold newspapers for a while and then 'e got a job as bellboy in one of them new 'otels in The Strand. Later 'e got in with the turf mob. I saw 'im one afternoon the summer before last at Epsom working the three card trick and 'e was looking as dapper as ever I'd seen 'im, with a grey bowler and check suit and that silver watch I told you about. You don't suppose—'

'We're leaving the watch out of it,' said Thackeray firmly. 'Tell me, Mr Brand, did you ever meet the boy's mother again?'

'Never to speak to, although I've seen 'er once or twice in cabs. She moved out of Russell Square a long while back and I'm not sure where she went.'

'Did your son ever meet his mother?'

'Not while 'e was a boy, Officer, but I rather think it might 'ave crossed 'is mind last year to try and find 'er. When I saw 'im that afternoon on the race-course we talked about old times over a glass of ale – we was on very good terms, you see – and, seeing that 'e was now a man of the world, I told 'im the story I've just told you. Up to then 'e'd always believed 'is ma died of cholera. 'E seemed uncommon pleased to learn she was still alive, and asked me the number of the 'ouse in Russell Square. Of course I told 'im it was no good going there now because she's long since moved. I suppose 'e might 'ave called and found out the new address, but lately 'e's been very busy with the spirits and I 'aven't spoken to 'im since that afternoon at

Epsom. If you ask me, I don't reckon 'e got much of a welcome from 'er if 'e did find the place where she lives. She don't want to be reminded of us, I'm sure of that. Well, Officer, that's my story and I've rambled on for long enough.' He put his pipe in his pocket and struggled out of the armchair. 'I'll just 'elp you look through that chest of drawers and then I'm on my way. I work from the Charing Cross rank these days. You can always find me there if anything worth 'aving turns up.'

'It ain't so simple as that,' Thackeray explained. 'He might have made a will.'

'Couldn't write,' said Brand Senior.

'Well, his mother has the right to claim some of his possessions.'

This was a thought that had not occurred to the cabman. After a moment's reflection he shook his head. 'She's not going to come forward after all this time. She's in clover already. She's got no use for silver watches and check suits.' He opened the drawers one by one and passed his hand rapidly between the layers of socks and shirts. 'But if she wants any of this stuff she's welcome to it.'

'You didn't mention her name,' said Thackeray.

'No I didn't. One thing you learn in my occupation, Officer, is to be careful over names. There's passengers that like to be recognized and there's those that don't. Most times it's best to keep off names, so I never asked 'er what it was.'

'But you found it out, surely?'

'That's another matter. If I did, all the cab 'orses I've ever owned wouldn't drag it out of me.'

'Perhaps this would,' suggested Thackeray on an inspiration. He plunged his hand in his pocket – and came out

117

with four sixpences and a halfpenny. 'I could get some more by this afternoon,' he added lamely.

'I'll believe that when I see it,' muttered the cabman as he started downstairs.

Thackeray stood where he was, looking bleakly at the five coins in his palm. He would cheerfully have given a pound of his own money to have got that name and dumbfounded Cribb for once in his career. With a sigh he put the money back in his pocket, took out his notebook and started making the list of Peter Brand's possessions.

9

How would you treat such possibilities?
Would not you, prompt investigate the case . . .?

Sergeant Cribb was on a small square of carpet in front of Inspector Jowett's desk at Great Scotland Yard. He was standing at attention, motionless, so far as one could see. Actually his toes were wriggling in his boots.

'You know me for the last person in the world to discourage initiative,' Jowett was saying. 'My word, yes, I can claim with some pride that my record in assigning responsibility to the lower ranks is second to none in the Force. Consider, Sergeant, how often I have put you in charge of a murder inquiry, given you your head, so to speak, whilst I for my part have been content to take only that unobtrusive interest in events which you are entitled to expect from your superior. And of course you have always known that you can look in this direction for the support, the wisdom, the inspiration, the shaft of light that makes everything clear when all is darkest. I do not deny that there have been times when I was tempted to join you at the scene of a crime, to exercise my powers of deduction again, and with a few modest observations render hours of painstaking interrogation and inquiry unnecessary. My

119

place is here, however, in this office, overseeing not óne investigation alone, but up to a dozen simultaneously.' He tapped the side of his head with the mouth-piece of his pipe. 'This is the repository of sufficient information to bring sleepless nights to some of the blackest fiends in criminal London, Cribb. Yes, indeed, the Director cannot spare me to ferret out particular offenders. I am here to take the longer view.' To emphasize his point the inspector got up, walked to the window, cleaned a small section of it with the end of his thumb and peered out.

Cribb remained where he was, staring at the blank wall ahead, taking the shorter view appropriate to his rank.

'The other evening, however,' Jowett continued, 'a situation arose in which I was thrust willy-nilly into the investigation of a death in mysterious circumstances, upon a social occasion, among acquaintances for the most part unaware of my official position until I was compelled to declare it. Your unheralded arrival in Dr Probert's library made it quite impossible for me to remain in the room without revealing my connection with the Yard, but I do not blame you for that, Sergeant. You were pursuing an important suspect at the time. No, what concerns me about the events of Saturday evening was the manner in which you conducted yourself after the discovery of Mr Brand's death.'

Cribb frowned. What was Jowett complaining about – disrespect for the dead, intimidation of witnesses or ungenteel language? He was ready to admit them all. It was the only way with Jowett.

'I am not used to being brushed aside by anyone, Cribb, least of all a sergeant in my own command, but that is what happened the other evening, and in a private home, in polite company. I had not managed to articulate half-a-dozen questions before you started upon your theories about electricity, not to mention the advice to Dr Probert on the supervision of his domestic staff. It was acutely embarrassing, Sergeant, and tantamount to insubordination.'

Not only did Cribb's toes twitch; his knees jerked. 'Insubordination, sir?'

'Insubordination,' repeated Jowett, still looking out of the window. 'An officer of my rank expects to question witnesses without being interrupted by a detective-sergeant. The circumstances, I concede, were a little irregular, so on this occasion I may decide not to write a report to the Director, but be in no doubt that such conduct will not be countenanced a second time. Besides—' he turned from the window with a petulant look in his eye '– *I* could have thought of all those questions myself.'

'And wrapped 'em up in better words, sir,' said Cribb, quick to see the opening. 'I went quite beyond myself on Saturday, sir. Got carried away. Didn't realize you were wanting to do things in your own way. I'll hold myself in check in future.'

It earned him a grudging nod from Jowett. 'Very well, Cribb. Let us hopefully consider this matter closed. Do you know why I asked you to report to the Yard this afternoon?'

'For a parley about Mr Brand's death, I would guess, sir.'

Jowett shook his head. 'A *conference*, Sergeant, a conference. This is a modern detective force, not the Bow Street Runners. Yes, I have invited two other gentleman to attend: Mr Cage, who is an authority on electrical matters and has been examining the apparatus at Richmond, and Dr Benjamin, the police surgeon, who attended the *post mortem* examination conducted by the Home Office Pathologist this morning. The official report will be issued later, of course, but Dr Benjamin should be able to tell us the salient points this afternoon. Now be so good as to call in Constable Thackeray.'

Were it not for its location, the conference might have been taken for another seance. Jowett actually sat with his hands palm downwards on the table, but that was from vanity; he liked it to be known that he went regularly to a manicurist. Mr Cage, slimly-built and with deep-set pale blue eyes any medium would have envied, was on his left. Dr Benjamin, more conventionally handsome, with a black moustache and a glint in his eye suggesting he was capable of getting in touch, though not perhaps with spirits, sat next to him, opposite Thackeray and Cribb. A clerk waited with pen poised at a desk in the corner of the room.

'Let us dispense with formalities, gentlemen,' suggested Jowett. 'Dr Benjamin, we are all desirous of knowing the results of the *post mortem* examination. Did you ascertain the cause of death?'

Dr Benjamin nodded. It was clear from the way he then produced a box from his pocket (which Thackeray for one moment imagined contained a souvenir of the morning's work) and took snuff, that he saw no reason to expand upon this response. The information would have to be prised from him.

'It was not from natural causes, I presume?' said Jowett.

'No.'

'There was a weakness in the heart, we understood.'

'Confirmed,' said Dr Benjamin.

'So that a moderate electric shock would have killed him,' Jowett continued.

'Possibly,' said the doctor.

'Did you not establish that?'

'No. Not moderate. Massive.'

At this Mr Cage jerked to life. 'Massive? Impossible. That apparatus could not have put more than twenty volts through the man. I checked it myself.'

'Then you're wrong,' said Dr Benjamin simply.

'Wrong?' repeated Cage as if he had not heard correctly. 'Perhaps you are not aware that I have given lectures upon electrical theory at the Universities of Oxford and Cambridge and in all the principal capitals of Europe. Dr Probert's apparatus was incapable of electrocuting a man. I stake my reputation on it.'

Jowett turned to Dr Benjamin. 'Then what evidence is there that Brand died of a massive electric shock?'

The doctor showed by his expression that he regarded the question as a breach of etiquette. He had named the cause of death; that ought to be enough for a set of policemen. He tersely catalogued the findings. 'Severe contraction of the muscles, causing several splittings and fractures of the bones. Widespread destruction of tissues, including necrosis of areas of muscle and certain internal organs.'

'Quite impossible!' insisted Cage. 'Injuries on that scale could only have been caused by a force of several hundred volts. I have myself sat in the chair with the power turned on and felt no untoward effects.'

'The transformer that Dr Probert constructed did provoke some comment,' said Jowett, with a glance at Cribb. 'Could it have been faulty, and so transmitted the full current to the chair?'

'I subjected the transformer to a series of tests in my own laboratory,' said Cage, 'and I can assure you that there is no fault in the construction. I shall tell the coroner so on oath. I have science on my side, gentlemen.'

'I have an electrocuted corpse on mine,' retorted Dr Benjamin.

Jowett interposed a cough. 'We appear to have reached an impasse, gentlemen. I do assure you both that your findings are not in doubt. Somehow we have to find an explanation which fits all the evidence, and I begin to suspect that it might be something quite extraordinary. You see, gentlemen, I have the advantage over all of you, in that I was present from the start of the seance that preceded Mr Brand's death. My fellow-officers here will attest that I have both feet on the ground – I am speaking figuratively, for Heaven's sake, Thackeray – and I am not given to flights of imagination or hallucinations.'

Cribb, who was determined not to commit himself to anything approaching insubordination, nodded once.

'But I tell you,' Jowett went on, 'that in that seance I saw a spirit hand hovering in the air, a moving disembodied hand, blue in colour, shining luminously through the darkness. Others saw it as well, and two at least were touched by it. Later, fruit was thrown about the room, overturning a vase of flowers. I did not imagine these things, gentlemen. I am a senior police officer, trained to observe accurately. The things I saw on Saturday night at Dr Probert's convinced me that this spiritualism, for all its dubious practitioners, is not lightly to be dismissed. If there is such a thing as a genuine medium, Peter Brand was one. On Saturday, however, the spirit he was contacting appeared to be hostile. Oranges, as I mentioned, were flung at one of the sitters.' Jowett lowered his voice. 'I hesitate to say this within Scotland Yard itself, but I am almost disposed to think, in the absence of any rational explanation, that the death of Mr Brand was induced by a supernatural agency.'

'A hostile spirit, do you mean?' said Cage.

'If you insist, yes,' said Jowett. 'There are unknown forces just as powerful as electricity, we may be sure.'

'Poppycock!' said Dr Benjamin.

'I beg your pardon,' said Jowett.

'Supernatural agency be blowed!' said Dr Benjamin. 'Brand was a charlatan. Have you never heard of Blue John?'

'Blue John? He is not known to me.'

'It's a substance, not a person.'

'I am at a loss to understand what you are talking about, Doctor.'

'That's obvious. Before the *post mortem* we were asked to pay particular attention to the hands of the deceased. On examination we found a number of minute particles adhering to the surface of the right palm. When we analysed them they proved to be crystals of calcium fluoride, or fluor-spar – in layman's language, Blue John. There is a quick method of identifying the fluoride ion, which we carried out, heating the substance in concentrated sulphuric acid and holding a plate of clear glass over it. The hydrofluoric acid so produced etched the glass, rendering it opaque. Blue John, without a doubt.

Jowett was still shaking his head. 'I fail to see—'

Dr Benjamin turned his eyes heavenwards, inviting everyone round the table to share his exasperation at Jowett's incomprehension. 'When Blue John is gently heated,' he said, as if talking to a child, 'he glows in the dark. Have you not heard of fluorescence? The spirit hand you saw was the medium's, coated with fluor-spar, which he had warmed at the fire before the seance commenced. And if you don't believe that established Brand as an imposter, you might reflect on the fact that under his normal clothes he was wearing a nightshirt, in the pocket of which we found a small bag of talcum powder. You obviously have a closer acquaintance with the spirits than I, but I believe that people who have encountered them have observed that in their manifested form they have white faces and long, flowing garments.'

Jowett was pale enough to have slipped on a nightshirt himself and caused havoc in the corridors of Scotland Yard. 'We are – er – deeply in your debt, Doctor. This is remarkable information. Greatly to be commended.'

'We can't claim much credit,' said Dr Benjamin. 'We were acting upon the suggestion contained in a note we received before the *post mortem*. It categorically requested us to examine the palms for Blue John.'

'Really?' said Jowett weakly. 'Did you discover who wrote the note?'

'It was one of your chaps, or we shouldn't have acted upon it. A Sergeant Cribb.'

'My Godfathers!' said Jowett. He turned to look at Cribb, who had seldom felt so uncomfortable.

'I say, was it you?' asked Cage. 'You're a quiet one, by Jove!'

'How the devil did you know about Blue John?' demanded Jowett.

Cribb had pledged himself to keep out of trouble by not saying a word.

'Speak up, man!' ordered Jowett.

That made it insubordination to remain silent. 'I spent a few months in Derbyshire when I was in the army, sir.

Blue John is also known as Derbyshire Spar. It's common there.'

'Well, you might have had the decency to stop me earlier, when I was talking about supernatural forces. Made me seem a confounded – never mind. This has been most instructive, of course, but it has brought us no nearer to ascertaining how Mr Brand met his death, unless the sergeant has some other information he has been keeping from us.'

Everyone looked in Cribb's direction. He was acutely conscious of the delicacy of his position. Jowett must on no account be led to suppose that his thunder had been stolen again. 'No information of any note, sir. Nothing more than a few theories.'

'We had better hear them,' said Jowett resignedly. 'Mine has collapsed, so we may as well put yours to the test.'

'I'm obliged to you, sir. It seems to me that if the electric chair works perfect now, as Mr Cage has indicated, it couldn't have been working perfect at the moment Brand was electrocuted. Something must have happened to make it dangerous, something that was put right afterwards. So I'd like to ask Mr Cage if there was any way in which the main current could be made to by-pass the transformer.'

'Only by disconnecting it and fastening the cable directly to the wires that were attached to the arms of the chair,' said Cage. 'Or I suppose another way might be to attach a wire to the positive terminal on the mains side of the transformer and connect it on the other side with one of the trailing wires. In either case it would have to be a deliberate act and it would amount to murder.'

'Murder by electrocution,' mused Dr Benjamin. 'I've never heard of such a thing, but I suppose it's possible. Who would want to murder a medium?'

'Before we answer that,' said Jowett, 'there's a question I should like to put to Mr Cage. If some malevolent person chose to tamper with the apparatus in one of the ways you have described would he not run the risk of electrocuting himself?'

'If he tried it when the power was on, he would certainly kill himself,' Cage confirmed.

Jowett spread his palms to signify the collapse of Cribb's theory.

'As I understood it,' returned Cribb, looking steadily at the table in front of him as he spoke, 'there was an interruption during the seance when Mr Brand claimed that someone had entered the study. Mr Nye went downstairs to turn off the current. It was not turned on again until Mr Brand was pacified. Shortly after, Brand was found dead in the chair.'

'That is so,' conceded Jowett, discountenanced again.

'What I can't explain is why he was not killed at the instant the power was restored,' Cribb went on. 'If I have it correct, the experiment was set up again at twenty minutes to eleven, the current was switched on and the galvanometer reading was not exceptional. It was a full minute before the needle jumped and we pulled aside the curtain to find Brand's body.'

'It makes no sense to me,' said Cage.

'There's a notion forming at the back of my mind, but it'll want time,' said Cribb. 'For the present, can we proceed upon the assumption that this was murder?'

'If you think it will lead us somewhere,' said Jowett, without much enthusiasm.

'Well, sir, let's return to the spirit hand for a moment.'

Jowett went a shade pinker.

'If Brand was waving his right palm, coated with Blue John, about in the air – and it must have looked uncommon convincing, sir – he couldn't have been holding the hand of the person on his right. In other words, the circle was broken and that person must have known it and been a party to the deception.'

'By George, yes!' said Jowett. 'Do you know who it was? Miss Crush, of all people! I am absolutely certain of it.'

'Rightly so, sir. Mr Strathmore very helpfully made a plan of the seating arrangements, which I borrowed on Saturday. Miss Crush, as you say, sat on the right of the medium and must have helped him. Now why should that lady be so rash as to conspire with a fraud – as we now know Brand to have been? He was not her class of person at all. You don't find respectable maiden ladies with houses in Belgravia associating with the dregs of the race-course. There had to be some reason for this irregular alliance.'

'I think I know it, Sarge,' said Thackeray suddenly.

'We'll return to you in a moment, then,' said Cribb without much gratitude. 'I first suspected something between them when we attended Professor Quayle's lecture. Already she had tried to persuade me not to question Peter Brand about the theft of her vase, although at the time I put that down to her enthusiasm for spiritualism, and her wish not to upset the medium. But at the lecture, it was crystal clear that she was there to help him, supplying him with information about Uncle Walter, and pretending it was all quite new, although they had been through the same performance at the first seance at Richmond.'

'A point that had eluded me, Sergeant,' said Jowett. 'It may be significant!'

'It seemed likely that the medium had got some hold on Miss Crush and was using her to further his career. The first seance was held at her house in Eaton Square, if you recall, sir. I couldn't fathom what the secret was, or how Brand came to possess it.'

'I could tell you, Sarge,' offered Thackeray.

'All in good time, Constable. But on the night the medium met his death it all became clear. Do you remember how Miss Crush behaved, sir?'

'We had to restrain her from going to him in the chair, as I recollect,' said Jowett. 'And after that she was repeatedly fainting, confounded woman. Now that you bring it to my attention it was curious behaviour. It would certainly indicate that there was a bond of some description between them.'

'That's exactly what I thought, sir, though I couldn't have put it so elegant. The clincher was in the wallet we found on his body. Do you remember when we made the list of his possessions?'

'I have it with me,' said Jowett, producing a notebook from his pocket as proudly as a plumber's mate putting his hands on the required spanner.

'I though I could rely on that, sir. Do you have a note of those numbers we found on the reverse of the photograph?'

'Yes, indeed. 469 and 9281, followed by the symbol of a square. Do they have something to do with the young woman *in puris naturalibus* on the other side?'

'That was my first thought,' said Cribb, 'but I racked my brains for an hour or more and couldn't see a connection. Then I looked more closely at the photograph. It was somewhat creased and dog-eared, if you remember. It must have been kept in his wallet for some considerable time. Yet it wasn't the sort of picture a man might carry in his wallet out of sentiment.'

'I doubt whether the female in the photograph was his sister or his fiancée, if that is what you mean.'

'That's exactly what I mean, sir. There's a row of shabby little shops in Holywell Street, just off The Strand, which purvey photographs like that by the hundred. They call 'em art studies, and Inspector Moser goes there periodically with a couple of his men and seizes the most offensive specimens. There are always new ones to replace 'em, though, and if one dealer comes to court there's another to take his place. The photographs themselves have been getting more objectionable of late. I believe they ship 'em in from France on the cross-Channel steamers; you wouldn't catch any of the fair sex here taking up such brazen attitudes in front of a photographer. But you'll know yourselves, as gentlemen of the world, that the men who buy these things are forever searching for something new. They don't keep them for any length of time. That's what's so odd about the photograph in Peter Brand's wallet. It's been there too long. In the end I was forced to conclude that he didn't keep it all that time for the lady on the front, but for the numbers on the back. They had an importance of their own. And when I thought of 'em in isolation they began to make sense.'

'I don't know how,' said Cage. 'May I look at them, Inspector?'

'What you must realize as you study them,' said Cribb, 'is that Brand was an illiterate. We came to that conclusion some days ago at a lecture given by Professor Quayle.'

Jowett looked blank, but said nothing. Thackeray said, 'Illiterate, Sarge?'

'He couldn't read,' explained Cribb. 'When Brand came on to the stage during the lecture to do his turn it was Quayle who read out the names written on the envelopes containing articles borrowed from the audience. At one stage Brand was holding your envelope in his hand and he had to *ask* Quayle what the name was.'

'So he did!' recalled Thackeray in admiration.

'But if he didn't know his letters, at least he was cognisant of numbers or he wouldn't have kept the photograph. It was when I looked at those numbers trying to pretend I was as illiterate as Brand that I understood their meaning. They were the two most important numbers in his life.'

'How on earth do you deduce that?' said Jowett.

'By taking the second number first. It's the one with the square beside it, and that's helpful. I had to say it to myself a dozen times before I got it. 9281 square. You say the digits one by one, as an illiterate would. 9 and 2 are numbers, but 8 and 1 are words, eight one, the nearest he could get in numbers to Eaton. It's an illiterate's way of writing 92, Eaton Square. And that, if you remember, sir, is Miss Crush's address in Belgravia.'

'Eight one square,' said Jowett. 'It doesn't sound like Eaton Square to me.'

'Not the way you say it, sir,' conceded Cribb. 'But Peter Brand wasn't taught to speak the way you was. Let's hear you say Eaton, Thackeray.'

'Eaton,' said Thackeray with more than usual care.

'I take your point, Cribb. But if that set of digits represents Miss Crush's address, what is the significance of the others? 469 doesn't sound like anything to me and I don't think it would even if Thackeray said it.'

'It stands for the other important person in his life, sir.

I looked it up in the Hackney Carriage Licensing Department. 469 is the licence number of one Charles Brand, cabman.'

'His father! Good Lord! Are you suggesting that Miss Crush might be his—'

'Must be, sir. I'll be confirming it this evening. Now, Thackeray, you had something to contribute, I believe.'

Thackeray had parted with ten shillings, for the same information on the Charing Cross cab-rank that morning, but now he shook his head. 'I think you've said all there is to say, Sarge.'

In the interests of decorum Miss Crush had left her bed, in which she had been confined in a state of shock since Saturday with orders that the servants were not to disturb her except for meals. She had put on a black velvet dressing-robe and positioned herself on the chaise-longue in her drawing-room. Cribb, who had adventitiously arrived as the apple charlotte was going upstairs, sat at a discreet distance in an upright chair and expounded his theories much as he had at Scotland Yard, with some concessions to the delicate state of his listener.

'I *knew* that you were a sensitive,' said Miss Crush when he had finished. 'Didn't I recognize you as one the first moment you came into my house? You can look into a woman's eyes and see the secrets of her life laid bare, can't you? Oh, they must have jumped for joy at Scotland Yard the day they recruited you, Sergeant.'

'I don't recall it, ma'am,' said Cribb. 'But I think you should understand that I didn't uncover these personal matters through guess-work. It was a process of deduction.'

'Seduction?' said Miss Crush. 'Oh no, it was not that. I

might have been an *ingénue* twenty years ago, but I was not so ill-bred as to allow myself to be seduced by a common cabman, I seduced *him*.'

'You did, ma'am?' said Cribb, grateful for this unsolicited information.

'I did, most certainly. I was one of the New Women. It was the time when dear Mr Mill was holding up the banner of emancipation. I listened to a speech he made in the election of 1865 and it transformed my life, Sergeant. I decided on the spot that I should never be the slave of man and I have not faltered in that resolution since. But so that I should know what I was to devote my life to fighting against, namely the power man has to enslave my own poor sex, I resolved to make one foray into the enemy camp. If I got to know the contents of his armoury he would be powerless ever to take me by stealth, you see. It was sound strategy as you must appreciate.'

'Very sound, ma'am.'

'I had to choose a man of suitable age and physical attributes, but of course it needed to be someone quite outside my social circle. That made it very difficult, but then I had an inspiration. There were rows of men sitting on view at every cab-rank in London. I took a walk along The Strand one morning and selected a subject at my leisure.'

'Number 469.'

'That was he. I noticed that his horse – which I think he called Deuteronomy or something from the Bible – was conspicuously underfed, even for a cab-horse, so I made that the reason for my interest. I sent my servant back to hire him and that was the first of several excursions in the cab.'

134

'Several, ma'am?' said Cribb, lifting an eyebrow.

'It was necessary to undermine his defences first, Sergeant.'

'Of course,' said Cribb. 'Did you – er – gain access to the armoury?'

'Within a week. It was the only occasion I assure you, but unhappily for my plans there was a consequence.'

'Young Brand?'

'Yes. In the true emancipating spirit I made quite sure that it was his father who raised him. I provided money for his upkeep until he was old enough to earn for himself.' Miss Crush sighed. 'I am afraid the boy was shamefully neglected. If I had thought there would be a child I should have selected a cabman with a better looking horse. People who treat animals well are usually tolerant of children. The truth of it is that the boy got into odious company, thieves and tricksters and probably worse. I believe his father lost touch with him altogether.'

'You lost touch too, I gather, ma'am.'

'Goodness, yes. It would have been most imprudent of me to have anything to do with the boy. He thought I died of cholera when he was a child. He thought so at least until one afternoon last year, when he met his father on a race-course and the silly man must have drunk far too much, because he told Peter the whole story. The rest must be obvious to a man of your insight. Peter took some months to trace me, but he did, early this year. It was a terrible shock, Sergeant, unforgettable. Oh, he was very charming in his way, and disarming too. From his unwholesome friends he had acquired the art of winning a lady's confidence, as I learned to my cost. Weeks passed before he suggested anything irregular, but for him the time was not wasted. He used those weeks, I now realize, to learn about my way of life, my friends and my social engagements. He took particular interest in the seances I attended and he made me tell him everything that happened, time and again. Foolishly I allowed myself to be flattered by his interest, and I never tired of answering his questions. You can see what was happening, can't you? I see it in your eyes.'

'It's the way these people work, ma'am. We get to know their methods.'

'Well, one evening he suggested we should play a prank on my friends, the Bratts. Sir Hartley and his wife are somewhat elderly and Penelope, their daughter, is easily taken in. The plan was that I would arrange a seance, which was certain to interest them because they like nothing better than to get in touch, and I would introduce Peter as a medium. With my help he would then produce some marvellous phenomena. At first I would not agree, on the grounds that it was uncharitable, and might even provoke hostility on the Other Side, but Peter said it was like a parlour-game, and there was no harm in it. He promised never to attempt anything of the kind in a genuine seance. In short, Sergeant, he was so enthusiastic that I found it impossible to disincline him from the plan. We invited the Bratts, and they were totally convinced that he was genuine! The pity of it was that the deception did not end there. He made me introduce him to more of my friends in the spiritualist movement and he repeated his performance, never telling them, of course, that what we did was fraudulent. It is a strange thing, but the more mystified they were, the more impossible it became to tell them the truth. It would have upset them so.'

'I can see that,' said Cribb.

'In a surprisingly short time he was beginning to gain a reputation as a successful medium. I believe he appeared at houses in other parts of London and produced some quite extraordinary phenomena, which I can only presume were engineered with the help of some of his vile acquaintances. He was not a genuine sensitive, I assure you of that. Well, Sergeant, the rest of the story I need hardly recount. Peter became established as the most gifted medium in London and everyone was clamouring to engage him. I confess to you that I participated fully in his deceptions: I pretended to see and hear phenomena that never occurred; I simulated rapping sounds under the table by knocking the heels of my boots together; and I carried things for him under my clothes and passed them to him during the sittings.'

'What kinds of things were they, ma'am?'

'Ah, you are thinking of what we in the movement call "apports", Sergeant, objects that miraculously appear during seances. At times a seance table has been known to be entirely covered by flowers or fruit introduced by the spirits. But Peter would have nothing to do with apport phenomena. He said that it was too open to assertions of trickery. The only objects I carried for him were small boxes containing chemicals which he used to produce luminous effects.'

'Were you carrying one of them for him on the night of his death?'

'No. By then he had refined his methods. Anything he used in his more recent appearances he carried himself.'

'He had fluor-spar on his hand, ma'am, but we found no box upon him. What did he do with it, do you think?'

'I believe he must have chosen the time before the seance

began to spread the chemical over his hand. Then all he had to do was throw the empty box into the fire. He needed to stand near the fire to heat the substance on his hand. If you remember, he placed a fire-screen in the grate shortly before the seance began. Any small amount of the chemical still in the box would not have been noticed burning.'

Cribb nodded. 'That sounds to me like the way he did it, ma'am. It would have seemed quite innocent at the time, even if someone had noticed him. You didn't carry anything for him on Saturday evening, then?'

'Nothing at all, Sergeant. My participation was limited to claiming that I could sense the presence of a spirit and that it actually touched me. And, of course, I was sitting next to Peter so that he could break the link in the chain of hands to produce the various effects.'

'You weren't the only one who claimed to have been touched. Alice Probert said she felt a spirit hand upon her. That was the occasion for Captain Nye's outburst, I believe.'

'I cannot answer for Miss Probert or Captain Nye,' Miss Crush primly answered.

'I suppose not. Did your son – did Peter Brand throw the oranges at Captain Nye himself?'

'I can assure you that *I* didn't throw them, Sergeant.'

'I'm sure you didn't,' said Cribb hastily, 'but I don't believe a spirit visitor threw them either, and from what you tell me of Brand's methods I don't think he would resort to anything as crude as that. You don't suppose that someone else had broken the link in the chain as well as yourself?'

'I don't know what to suppose,' said Miss Crush. 'A number of things happened that evening that I find very difficult to account for, but *supposing* isn't going to help, is it? You *know* what happened, anyway, don't you?'

Cribb ignored the question. 'There's one thing more, Miss Crush. I believe that you are quite well known in what you call the spiritualist movement.'

'I flatter myself that I am, Sergeant. I have devoted myself to it with all the energy I lavished on the women's movement in my youth.'

'The thing that puzzles me, ma'am, is why you went so far with Peter Brand in his deceptions. It was one thing to play a joke on the Bratts, but quite another to create a fraudulent seance in Dr Probert's house in front of an investigator from the Life After Death Society. These men were scientists, ma'am, seekers after truth. Sooner or later they were going to find you out and it was certain to destroy your reputation. As well as that, it would do irreparable harm to the cause of spiritualism.'

'I was well aware of that, Sergeant. There have been exposures enough of fraudulent mediums in recent years. The movement could not afford another.'

'Then why did you persist with it?'

'Why do you ask me what is obvious? I had no choice, I was under threats from my son. He was blackmailing me, Sergeant. If I didn't help him in his infamous deceptions he would have told the world what happened twenty years ago between a cabman and a rather rash disciple of Mr John Stuart Mill.'

Before Cribb left Eaton Square that evening he looked back through the trees at the long white terrace, its windows ablaze with light, spacious windows draped with elegant curtains. Behind them was what Miss Crush called 'the world', and it was not difficult to imagine how her youthful indiscretions would have been received there if she had refused to submit to Brand's blackmail. She was undeserving of pity; he knew that he had only to pass a few hundred yards south-west into Ebury Street and look at the dimly-lit windows of Pimlico with their cheap hangings to banish any pangs he might feel on Miss Crush's account. But he understood her, and that was what mattered. And he detested blackmail in any form. It was indefensible, whatever the victim might have done. It could also provide a motive for murder.

10

A right mood for investigation, this!

As a corpse, Thackeray was less than satisfactory. There were plenty in the Force more lean, pale and passably cadaverous than he. Years of beat-pounding by night left some officers looking like that, while others seemed to put on flesh and get redder in the face with every duty they were ordered to perform. Thackeray was among the latter, and this morning he was the only one available.

'You might at least try not to look so comfortable in the chair,' complained Cribb. 'The body was rigid when we found it, and the hair was standing on end.'

'Sorry, Sarge. Electrocutions are something new in my experience.'

The apparatus was now restored to its original position in the library, Dr Probert's transformer having passed all the tests Mr Cage had devised for it. Cribb had been assured that the chair was in good working order. No more than twenty volts could possibly pass through the body of anyone who gripped the handles when the current was switched on.

Cribb had a vivid recollection of the position and appearance of Peter Brand when they had pulled back the curtain on the night of the tragedy, and he was doing his best to recreate the scene with Thackeray's assistance. Mr Etty must have gone through a not dissimilar procedure each time he set the model in position for the *Sleeping Nymph and Satyrs*. Mr Etty, of course did not have Thackeray to sit for him, but it was Cribb's opinion that if Thackeray was posing for you it did not matter much whether your subject was a sleeping nymph or a dead medium; you were defeated before you started.

'You're still too central,' he said, regarding Thackeray out of one eye, as if using two would cause him distress. 'Turn your legs to the right and get your back into the left hand side of the chair and bring your weight forward.'

Thackeray wriggled helpfully.

'That's more like it. What are you holding the handles for?'

'He must have been holding the handles to get an electric shock, Sarge.'

'He *should* have been,' said Cribb. 'The muscles contract at the moment of shock. His hands should have taken an iron grip. But they didn't. His left arm was hanging down on the left side of the chair. You've raised an interesting point there, Thackeray.'

'Thank you, Sarge,' beamed Thackeray. Praise from Cribb was too rare to pass unacknowledged.

'Well, get your arm down, man! Didn't you hear what I said?'

The beginning of a theory was forming in Cribb's brain. If Brand had moved his left hand off the handle, perhaps to tamper with the transformer behind him, and alter the connexions of the wires in some way, might he not have touched the positive terminal in error and electrocuted himself?

'See if you can touch the transformer from there, Thackeray. You'll need to slide further down than that and get your armpit over the chair-arm.'

Thackeray manoeuvred his rump towards the front of the chair and stretched behind with his arm, like a prize-fighter reaching from his corner for a bracer. Unhappily for the theory, his fingers stopped some inches short of the transformer; and unless Brand had got the physique of a gorilla, his arm must have been shorter than Thackeray's.

Cribb frowned and got on his knees to check that the chair and transformer were correctly placed. Mr Strathmore had efficiently marked the carpet with chalk shortly after the body had been taken from the chair. The present positions corresponded exactly with the outlines.

Before Cribb got up, he picked two small filmy wisps from the carpet near the transformer and held them in the palm of his hand.

'What have you found, Sarge?' asked Thackeray.

'They look like flower petals to me,' said Cribb. 'Chrysanthemums probably. There was a vase of them turned over next door.'

'Somebody must have brought them in on his shoes,' suggested Thackeray.

'Possibly,' said Cribb, placing them carefully between the leaves of his notebook. 'Are you quite sure you can't touch the transformer from there?'

'It's impossible,' Thackeray declared. 'Besides, I've thought of something else, Sarge. If he was reaching behind like this, he must have broken contact with the circuit, and that would have been recorded on the dial next door.'

'That's a fair observation,' said Cribb, 'but what you must remember is that Peter Brand wasn't noted for playing fair.

A man used to working the three card trick isn't going to let two scientists and a galvanometer get the better of him. If he wanted to free his hand he had only to rest his chin on the handle, and the contact would remain unbroken. Try it.'

Thackeray's face was already practically in contact with the handle. By turning it an inch or two to the left he achieved the position Cribb had described.

'The strength of the contact would have changed, of course,' Cribb went on, 'but they were looking for a *break* of contact on the galvanometer, and that didn't happen because he didn't take his hand off the handle until his chin was in contact. From what I've heard from Inspector Jowett there were several variations in the readings, but nothing suspicious enough to bring anyone in here until the needle suddenly indicated a complete break of contact. When we pushed aside the curtain he was dead from a huge electric shock and his hand, or whatever part of him it was that came in contact, had been forced clear by the contraction of the muscles.'

'It couldn't have been his hand, Sarge. Look, mine couldn't possibly reach the transformer,' said Thackeray, demonstrating by pawing the air with his left hand a good six inches short of the deadly terminal on the cable side of the transformer.

'If it comes to that,' said Cribb, 'there ain't any part of his body that could have reached that far, unless he was a contortionist as well as a card-sharp. But he must have touched *something* that gave him a lethal shock.'

'It's a regular conundrum, Sarge,' said Thackeray, with his knack of articulating the obvious. 'May I take my chin off the handle now? My beard's itching fit to break my concentration.'

Cribb nodded. 'We won't learn any more from the chair anyway. There must be something else in all this, Thackeray, something we haven't considered at all. Let's look at it from Brand's point of view. He knows in advance that he's going to have to do some clever stuff to pull the wool over the scientists' eyes, so he comes prepared. He brings Blue John, which he uses for the first seance, and he wears a nightshirt under his clothes ready to fake a materialization in the second half of the evening. But is that enough?'

'It don't seem very much,' said Thackeray. 'I'm sure I wouldn't be taken in by *anyone* in a nightshirt.'

'Don't count on it,' warned Cribb. 'Suggestion is a powerful thing, Thackeray. They'd seen one apparition already that night, in the shape of a disembodied hand. They were sitting in near-darkness waiting for the next. I believe some of 'em took *me* for a ghost when I walked in – and I wasn't wearing a nightshirt. Take my word for it, you'd have been shaking in your boots like the rest of 'em.'

'I usually do if I meet you unexpected, Sarge.'

'Really?' said Cribb, momentarily disturbed. 'I can't think why. The point I was coming to is that if Brand knew in advance that he was going to be seated in this chair for an experiment, he would surely have devised some way of cheating.'

'How would he go about it, Sarge?'

'That's a question I'd rather not answer before I know whether the first assumption is correct. The way to find out whether Brand inspected this apparatus before last Saturday is to ask the Proberts.'

They were in the drawing-room across the hall where Cribb had first met them. Mrs Probert, whom he noticed first because he was determined not to overlook her this

145

time, was seated in her favourite place under the palm. Dr Probert was standing at the window looking out at the nannies doing perambulator duty on the Terrace. At the fireplace was Alice, dressed to go out in a dark green coat with a frogged front, and a large plush hat of the same colour with a dash of white in the trimming. She was adjusting it at the mirror.

'What do you want, man?' demanded Probert, without taking his eyes off the nannies.

'A little of your time, if it can be spared, sir – and ladies.'

'My daughter's just going out,' said Probert. 'It's a damned fool thing to be doing on a day like this, but she won't be told. Charity can't study the weather, she says. She'll die of pneumonia before she's twenty-five, while the great unwashed of Richmond grow old and get fat on the fruit and veg. she's given 'em.'

'It's not like that at all, Father,' said Alice, glancing into the mirror at Cribb. Her face had a doll-like neatness, with large blue eyes and high cheek-bones that gave the permanent promise of a smile. 'They certainly won't get fat on the meagre amount I provide. Letting them know that someone cares is what really matters. The food is a meagre gesture.'

'If that's all it is, let's keep the five shillings a week and have a bottle of champagne on Saturdays,' said Mrs Probert.

'Mama, that's a dreadful thing to say in front of the sergeant!' Alice chided her. 'Don't take any notice, Mr Cribb. You can't rely upon a quarter of the things she says.'

'If my arithmetic is right, that means three-quarters of the things I say are reliable,' said Mrs Probert without a glance in her daughter's direction. 'If the words of other people in this house – not to say their conduct – could be

146

relied upon to that extent, the sergeant would have an easier task.'

Alice turned from the mirror to look at her mother, an action insignificant in normal circumstances, but noteworthy in this family, whose members seemed to have evolved monolithic existences based on the least possible acknowledgement of each other's presence. 'What are you insinuating by that remark, Mother?'

Mrs Probert continued to look at the carpet. 'That's a bold new hat you are taking so much care over arranging, my dear. If the hat fits, wear it, I say,' she said mysteriously.

Alice indulged in another long look at Mrs Probert, a look singularly devoid of the regard a daughter might be expected to feel for her mother. Then she addressed Cribb. 'Wouldn't you prefer to speak to Papa in private?'

'Not at all, miss, but if I'm delaying you—'

'I can wait a few minutes.'

'In that case, miss, I'll presently escort you down the hill. I've got a constable sitting in the hall who can carry your gifts for the poor.'

'That's very obliging of you. It's a shopping-basket, you know, not the sort of thing one generally sees a policeman carrying.'

'Don't concern yourself, miss. I'll see that he keeps a respectable distance behind us. Now, Doctor, if I may . . .'

Probert turned at last from the window. 'What is the trouble then?'

The phrase came so readily that Cribb suspected it was the one the doctor used in consultations.

'No trouble at present, sir. I'm merely wanting to establish certain facts touching on the death of Mr Brand. That apparatus in the library, sir: when did you get it ready?'

'The chair, you mean? On Wednesday of last week, I believe. Strathmore came to help me. It didn't take long. We had to screw on the brass handles and connect the various wires, but to a scientist it's a very elementary piece of wiring. There really wasn't much to go wrong, which makes the accident all the more baffling.'

'It's a puzzle indeed, sir. Mr Strathmore helped you, you say?'

'Helped him drink his claret,' put in Mrs Probert.

'That was *after* we had set up the experiment,' said Probert, sensitive, for once, to an interruption from his wife. 'It's not done to offer muffins and tea to a professional acquaintance. The answer, Sergeant, is yes. Mr Strathmore helped me. It was fortunate as it turned out. We can both vouch for the safety of the apparatus. I believe your expert from the Home Office was unable to detect any fault in the wiring.'

'That's correct, sir.'

'The transformer was found to be in good order?'

'Perfect, sir.'

'I thought so. The wire and the galvanometer were new. I purchased them from Mr Cooper, who owns the supply station. It's a rum go, is all this. You know, I've been trying to decide whether it was Brand's dickey heart that did for him. He *looked* as though he'd been subjected to a powerful shock. I'd have staked my reputation on that, but I suppose twenty volts or so of electricity could be just as destructive to a chap in his condition as several hundred to you or me.'

'That may be so, sir, but it doesn't account for the fracturing of several of his bones. Do you mind if I continue with my questions? Did Mr Brand by any chance inspect the apparatus before Saturday night?'

'No,' said Probert firmly.

Alice turned from the mirror. 'But Papa—'

'Brand did not inspect the apparatus before Saturday night,' Probert insisted in a way that brooked no challenge from his daughter. 'Without wishing to denigrate Mr Brand, I think it must be obvious that he was not the class of person one invites to one's house except in a professional capacity.'

'I was thinking that for professional reasons he would have wished to come in advance, to view the room where the seance was to be held,' said Cribb.

'You have obviously forgotten that Brand came here previously for a seance,' said Probert. 'It was on October 31st, the night the vase was stolen from Miss Crush's residence. He had an ample opportunity then to inspect the room.'

'But he didn't see the chair before Saturday?'

'That is so. If we'd given the fellow a chance to make preparations, it would have invalidated the blasted experiment. Is the interrogation over?'

'For the present, sir, I'm obliged to you,' said Cribb as if it was a wrench to take himself away from such congenial company. 'Now, Miss Alice, where's that basket?'

Halfway down Richmond Hill, with Thackeray ten yards in the rear carrying a shopping basket topped with oranges, Alice Probert said to Cribb, 'You believe Peter Brand was murdered, don't you?'

'It's a possibility, miss.'

'Papa thinks so, too. He thinks Professor Quayle did it.'

'I thought he put it down to the weakness of Peter Brand's heart,' said Cribb.

'Oh, he wants to. That's the explanation that will cause the least offence all round. He doesn't want the opprobrium

149

of a public murder trial, with us all appearing as witnesses, but he is not such a fool as he seemed this morning, Sergeant. He knows very well that the shock that killed Mr Brand would have killed anyone sitting in that chair at that moment. He is quite convinced that somebody tampered with the apparatus.'

'And he suspects the professor?'

'Papa's argument is that Professor Quayle was the only person in the house that night with a motive for murdering Mr Brand – professional jealousy. That was the explanation of the burglaries, was it not?'

'Broadly speaking, yes, miss.'

'Well, my father reasons that the professor must have been the person who crept into the study while Mr Brand was sitting in the chair and caused him to call out and interrupt the seance.'

'I think he's correct in that, miss.'

'He believes that in those few seconds the professor did something to ensure that within a very short time Mr Brand would be subjected to a huge electric shock.'

'And what was that?'

She smiled, 'Papa doesn't know. He says that he is not a policeman. Of course, Mama and I have our own suspicions. We don't subscribe to Papa's theory at all.'

'No, miss?'

'No, we're perfectly sure that Professor Quayle is not a murderer. He's an old friend to us. We've known him for a long time, and he often visits us.'

Cribb's eyebrows shot up. 'Now that's a thing I didn't know.'

'Oh yes. Papa has been interested in spiritualism for at least ten years. He invited the professor home for dinner after he met him once at a lecture, and he calls socially quite often. When I was younger he always used to bring me sweets – pangoods and surprise packets – so I *can't* think of him as a murderer.'

'With respect, miss, I don't suppose you could think of him as a housebreaker either, but he is. He admits to it.'

'Yes, but he isn't a hardened criminal. You got the stolen things back, didn't you? I hope he gets a light sentence, poor duck. Mama is exceedingly upset about the whole episode.'

'I thought your mother disapproved of spiritualists. She didn't have much time for Peter Brand, if I understood her correct.'

'Oh, Professor Quayle is as different from Peter Brand as chalk from cheese. A charming man. Besides, he never discusses the spirits with Mama. She has a high opinion of him, I assure you. Do you like hot chestnuts? There's a man who sells them at the bottom of the hill, near the bridge.'

'It's a shade too early in the day, thank you,' said Cribb.

'I'll buy some for your man, then. I hate to walk straight past street-vendors, don't you? Mama is quite wrong about the spirits, of course. It's really awfully jolly to get in touch. William, my fiancé, isn't much better. He gets positively liverish when the lights go out.'

'So I've heard, miss. But *you* don't get alarmed, I gather. I understand you felt your clothes being tugged and your hair touched on Saturday, is that so?'

'It's not at all unusual in a seance,' said Alice, without really answering the question. 'There's no need to agitate oneself about such things, as William did.'

'Perhaps there's a natural explanation for what happened, anyway,' suggested Cribb.

'I trust not. What a disagreeable thought!' Alice's hand went to her hair and rearranged it over her collar.

'You're quite convinced that the spirits touched you on Saturday?' asked Cribb, determined to pin Miss Probert down.

'I'm sure it wasn't anybody else in the room.'

'But you're equally sure that it happened?'

'I don't imagine things, Sergeant.'

'No, miss.' It was the nearest he would get to an answer. They were fast approaching the chestnut stall, and he had something else to ask. 'You said just now that you and Mrs Probert have your own suspicions about Saturday. Might I inquire whom you suspect?'

'Mr Strathmore.'

'The scientist?'

'He is a dangerous man, Sergeant. Papa should never have associated with him. One looks for a degree of detachment in a scientist, a commitment to proceed by the scientific method of hypothesis, investigation and proof. When Mr Strathmore came to the house on Wednesday to prepare the experiment, he revealed himself as anything but detached. His sole object was to set traps and snares, in the conviction that the medium would fall victim to them and show himself to be fraudulent. If Papa had not been firm with him he would have smeared the handles of the chair with carbon so that anything the medium touched would be marked, and he had brought cotton thread with him to weave a giant cat's cradle around the room, if you please, in the belief that it would snap and prove the medium had left the chair. Imagine the impression such stratagems would have made on a medium of Mr Brand's standing!'

'It might have led to an ugly scene, miss.'

'Exactly. He was totally fanatical in his determination to prove Mr Brand a charlatan. It was odious to see the way he calculated the position of the chair to the nth degree, just as if he was Sweeney Todd, the infamous barber. It had to be so far back from the curtain so that he couldn't lean forward and touch it, and the transformer had to be out of arm's reach, and the handles screwed in with screws an inch and a half in length. It makes me shudder to think of it now. He should be a public executioner, not a man of medicine.'

'That may be so, miss, but I can't arrest him for that. What you've told me doesn't endear Mr Strathmore to me, but none of it's against the law.'

'Don't you see, Sergeant? He and Papa were the only ones who knew what the chair looked like before Saturday. Between Wednesday and Saturday he must have thought of something else, some horrible appendage to the experiment that turned the chair into an execution-chair the moment poor Mr Brand moved his arm or shuffled his foot.'

'What sort of appendage exactly, miss?'

'I'm not certain, but then I'm—'

'Not a policeman, miss? That's not such a bad thing, if I might say so. Mr Strathmore and your father weren't the only ones who had a chance to see that chair before Saturday. From what you tell me, I'm bound to suppose that you saw it yourself. And if your mother agrees with you about Mr Strathmore, it's reasonable to presume that she saw it on Wednesday too. Now I gather also that Mr Nye is a frequent visitor to the house. Would it be too presumptuous to suppose . . .'

She smiled. 'All right, Sergeant. William saw it too, on Friday, when Mr Brand came—' She stopped, the colour rising in her cheeks.

They stood still by a pillar-box, only a few yards short of the chestnut stall, the fumes of burning nutshell and coke wafting towards them. 'Mr Brand, miss?' said Cribb. 'That's a funny thing. I rather supposed that he must have had a look at the apparatus, but your father didn't seem to remember the occasion. It was Friday, then.'

'Friday,' she confirmed in a low voice. 'He came to make arrangements about the seance.'

'That's understandable, miss.'

'Please don't let Papa know I told you. I really don't know why he was so unwilling to tell you about it.'

'It's our secret, miss. Hello, here's Thackeray. Miss Probert wants to buy you a bag of chestnuts, Thackeray.'

'That's very generous, miss.'

The chestnut man touched his cap as Alice approached him. She proffered twopence and said, 'I believe these gentlemen could catch a bus from here to Charing Cross, is that right?'

It was as neat a way as she could have contrived to terminate the interview.

'That's right, miss. Cost 'em a bob each.' He shovelled a large helping of chestnuts into a bag. Cribb stepped forward to take them, since Thackeray was still holding the basket and they were clearly too hot for a young lady to handle. He passed them to Thackeray in such a way that his back was towards Alice as he deliberately tore the side of the paper bag and dropped the still smoking nuts among the oranges in the basket.

'Moses, Sarge!' said Thackeray in bewilderment.

'Another bag, if you please,' called Cribb to the salesman.

It was the work of a few seconds to retrieve the hot nuts, and no visible damage was done to the fruit or the basket. To Thackeray it was a wholly mysterious incident, but he contained his curiosity until Miss Probert had set off again along Hill Street on her errand. 'Why did you do it, Sarge?' he asked, biting with relish into a chestnut.

'I wanted to see what was under that layer of oranges. Didn't you notice?'

'Yes, Sarge. A lady's hairbrush and comb. There's nothing extraordinary in that, is there?'

'That's a matter I want you to investigate, Constable. Follow Miss Probert and find out where she goes. You'd better leave the nuts with me, or she'll smell you coming a mile off.'

11

Now mark! To be precise –
Though I say, 'lies' all these, at the first stage,
'Tis just for science' sake:

Cribb had secured an inside seat between a large woman muffled in furs and a small boy occupied in scooping straw off the floor, shredding it and depositing pieces on the other passengers' clothes. It was not the best position on the bus, but it was preferable to the knifeboard upstairs. Common courtesy threatened to deprive him of his seat before long; there was sure to be some shopgirl late for work waving the driver down in Kew or Turnham Green. But he had privately resolved to see the small boy sitting on his mother's lap first. With that satisfying thought, he started on Thackeray's bag of chestnuts.

He considered what he had learnt from Alice Probert. In some particulars she was not to be relied upon – notably her experiences with invisible hands – but this morning's revelation that Brand had visited the house on Friday had escaped her lips before she realized its significance. Her consequent embarrassment had been genuine, no doubt of that. What she had said stamped Dr Probert as a liar.

He had firmly stated that Brand did not visit the house to examine the chair before Saturday.

The difficulty in dealing with Probert was that he was so easy to dislike. Cribb had handled him with kid gloves so far not because he was a friend of Inspector Jowett, but because antagonism towards a witness could lead to errors of judgement. It wanted guarding against. Probert was a liar, but that did not necessarily make him a murderer.

But why should he have lied at all about Brand's visit to the house? On the face of it, there was nothing sinister in a medium taking a preview of the place where he was to conduct a seance, particularly when the conditions were so unusual. It was questionable whether anyone would consent to being part of an electrical circuit without inspecting the apparatus first. People like Strathmore, dedicated to eliminating every possibility of fraud, might argue that seeing the apparatus in advance gave the medium the opportunity of devising some means of cheating science, but Cribb was not Strathmore; he was investigating a possible murder, not a manifestation. There were more important things at issue now than the validity of an experiment.

Obviously there was a reason why Probert did not wish it to be known that Brand had come to the house. The visit showed Probert – or someone he wished to protect – in an unfavourable light. It could well be connected with something Cribb had turned over in his mind repeatedly since the *post mortem*. There was reason to suspect that Dr Probert, like Miss Crush, had knowingly assisted Peter Brand in his deceptions.

Anyone unacquainted with Cribb's reasoning on this question could be forgiven for regarding the suggestion as monstrous. Would Probert have gone to the trouble of setting up an elaborate experiment in order to nullify its results by cheating? Cribb's understanding of events suggested exactly that. At the seance when the spirit hand had seemed to materialize, Probert had been seated next to the medium, holding his left hand. Was it not likely that whilst Brand's right hand, coated with Blue John, and helpfully liberated by Miss Crush, was describing convolutions in the air, slight pressures and tensions would have been transmitted by his left? And even if Probert could not *see* the rest of Brand's arm from so close a range, would he not have heard movements of his sleeve and shirt-cuff? More suggestive still were the oranges that had been flung at Nye. If it was accepted that they were not propelled by some supernatural agency, then either Miss Crush had thrown them with her left hand (an unlikely achievement), or Brand had used his right and nobody had noticed the Blue John on it (equally unlikely) or Dr Probert had something to do with it. The bowl containing the oranges had rested on a tripod table within reach of his right hand or Brand's left.

If Probert *had* conspired with Brand, there had to be an explanation for it. From what Cribb had learnt so far of Brand's *modus operandi* it was probably blackmail. And the chances were high that on the Friday evening when Brand had gone to Probert's house to view the apparatus, he had announced his terms. Some dark secret was to be preserved provided Probert, like Miss Crush, co-operated in producing spiritualistic phenomena.

The bus slowed to pick up a passenger, the brake-shoes rasping against the iron tyres. It was a nurse, probably bound for Charing Cross Hospital. Before she approached the platform, Cribb unpeeled the largest chestnut in the bag and offered it to the small boy. Just as the little fist was about to claim it, his mother whisked the child protectively on to her lap, and a seat was provided for the nurse.

It was difficult to imagine the sort of indiscretion that could have made Dr Probert susceptible to blackmail. Unlike Miss Crush, his standing in society was not threatened if a youthful peccadillo came to light. Nor was his marriage. That first conversation with Mrs Probert, before Cribb met the doctor, had convinced him that she was indifferent to her husband's extramarital distractions, whether they were naked goddesses or dancers from the music hall. No, it was some other thing with Dr Probert. Cribb had a shrewd idea that he would know what it was before the day was through.

For the rest of the journey he managed to retain his seat on the lower deck. From Turnham Green onwards his thoughts were on Mr Henry Strathmore, whom he had decided to interview next.

The *London Directory* gave the address of the Life After Death Society as Albemarle Street, as respectable a location as you could hope to find. The chambers were on the second floor, appropriately enough above the Veterans' Club. Cribb's knock was answered by a timid-looking young woman who explained that she was only the typewriter and Mr Strathmore was at lunch. She would be obliged if Cribb would come back at two o'clock. He consulted his watch. It was a quarter to two. He handed her his bowler and said he would wait.

'The gentleman insisted on waiting,' explained the typewriter apologetically when the door opened, exactly fifteen minutes later.

Strathmore jammed his monocle into place. 'I remember you. The gentleman from Scotland – er – won't you come into my office? Kindly step this way.'

His office would have been like any other but for the picture on the wall behind him. Instead of a portrait of the founder, it was a line-engraving of Daniel Home in horizontal levitation.

From the expression on his face Strathmore would dearly have liked to practise levitation himself at that moment, clean out of the window, down Albemarle Street and away along Piccadilly. 'What contingency has brought you to this office, Sergeant?' he asked.

'Mr Brand's death, sir,' said Cribb, as encouragingly as he could. 'Inspector Jowett has asked me to inquire into the circumstances.'

'Jowett, yes,' said Strathmore, as if something slightly offensive had been mentioned. 'You know, it was quite a shock to learn that Jowett was a peeler. I thought he was a senior Civil Servant at the very least.'

'I shouldn't let it depress you, sir. Inspector Jowett isn't one of your common peelers. He doesn't walk the beat at nights. He's got an office of his own and a house in South Norwood.'

'Has he, my word? I could see there was something genuine about the fellow. Mind you, I don't attach any importance to class, Sergeant. As a scientist, I cannot rule out the possibility that the spirits – if they exist at all—' He held up a cautionary finger '– might choose to communicate with us through a medium from the labouring class.' The finger altered in direction to point at the picture behind him. 'Daniel Home's father claimed to be the illegitimate son of the 10th Earl of Home, but the medium

160

was raised in quite modest circumstances.' He gave a thin smile, and added, 'Perhaps "reared" would be a happier choice of word than "raised" in his particular case.'

'For that matter, Mr Brand was only the son of a cabman,' Cribb observed, to bring the conversation down to earth, 'and he was getting invitations from some very well-connected people.'

'Yes indeed! There will be a few red faces in Mayfair and Belgravia when his deceptions are generally known. He is an example, I am afraid, of the axiom that breeding will out. I must admit that I had high expectations of Brand myself.'

'I remember, sir. You told me when I met you at Miss Crush's house.'

'Yes. Poor Miss Crush! She was completely taken in. As a scientist, of course, I took a more objective view of Brand. What a scoundrel he turned out to be! An imposter and an enemy of truth! The pity of it is that he enmeshed Professor Quayle in his infamous activities. I am quite sure that was the way of things, Sergeant. Quayle is at bottom a decent man, highly respected in spiritualistic circles. Brand corrupted him. He persuaded him to collaborate in his odious plot to rob the people whose houses he was visiting for seances. And now, you see, Quayle's own reputation is in ruins. Nobody will believe that he was ever an authentic medium. This appalling affair has set back the cause of spiritualism by at least ten years!'

This interpretation of events was somewhat at variance with Cribb's, but he had not interrupted because he saw no purpose at this stage in expounding theories of his own. Strathmore, for his part, had clearly needed to give vent to his feelings, and now looked ready to provide rational answers to questions.

'Would you describe yourself as a spiritualist, sir?'

'Good Lord, no! That would imply a commitment to the very things I am pledged to examine objectively. I am a scientist, no more and no less.'

'With respect, sir, the name of your society seems to suggest that the members have made up their minds already.'

'No more than the Ghost Club at Cambridge University, or the Society for Psychical Research. One has to provide some indication of what one proposes to investigate.'

'I take your point, sir. And you've been a member for twelve years, if I remember right.'

'Since 1873,' Strathmore confirmed.

'You must have investigated quite a little regiment of mediums in that time.'

'I think I can fairly state that I played some part in most of the inquiries the Society has initiated,' said Strathmore.

'I dare say you have seen some marvellous sights, sir.'

'Very few that I would dignify with that adjective, Sergeant. What might appear spectacular to the layman is of no interest to me if I can see that it is nothing more than a conjuring trick, as it usually is. If I have learned anything in these twelve years it is that the gullibility of the public is limitless.'

'You're still a sceptic yourself, are you, sir?'

'I am, Sergeant, until science shows me otherwise.'

'But you were prepared to take young Brand seriously?'

'Yes, indeed. We take every claim seriously until we have had the opportunity of testing it.'

'Did you know him personally, sir?'

'Not at all. It is usually better if we do not. My first contact with the young man was the seance at Dr Probert's on October 31st, the night that Professor Quayle took the opportunity of stealing Miss Crush's vase. I was sufficiently impressed with that seance to decide to take a second look at Brand, and that in itself is unusual. The phenomena, you see, were not exceptional – we heard some rappings and a spirit voice, as I recall – but they were singularly difficult to account for, although you must allow that it was in no sense a scientific experiment. That came later.'

'Was that your idea, or Dr Probert's?'

Strathmore took out his monocle and started polishing the lens. 'My recollection is that we were considering the possibility from the beginning, but we arranged for Brand to conduct the first seance in uncontrolled conditions to secure his co-operation. The Society has a clear policy over the matter of co-operation with mediums; we tell them exactly what the tests are to be. It really will not do to rip aside the curtains of cabinets or grab at the clothes of spirit forms. Science is capable enough of detecting fraud without melodramatic interventions of that sort.' He replaced the monocle firmly over his eye.

'So you devised the test with the electrical circuit,' said Cribb. 'Was that an apparatus you had used before, sir?'

'It was not. It was an invention of Probert's, but it promised to serve a useful purpose, so I co-operated in its construction.'

'You visited Dr Probert's house to assemble the experiment on Wednesday of last week, I believe.'

'I did, yes, but it seems an age ago now. I should like to emphasize that the apparatus was working perfectly at the end of Wednesday evening. We both took turns at sitting in the chair.'

'Were arrangements made for Mr Brand to see it before Saturday?'

'No, that was not necessary,' said Strathmore. 'He had agreed to put himself at the disposal of Science, so we showed it to him on Saturday at the commencement of the evening.'

'Would it surprise you to learn that he visited Dr Probert on Friday evening and inspected the chair then?'

Strathmore's monocle provided the answer to Cribb's question by dropping from his eye and landing with an alarming clink on the surface of his desk. When Strathmore added, 'Devious blighter!' it was by no means clear whether he was referring to Brand or Probert.

'I'd like to ask you about Saturday,' Cribb mildly went on. 'I've heard Inspector Jowett's account, of course, but I'd like to hear yours, sir, just in case there's something the inspector forgot. Have you by any chance prepared your report for the Society?'

'There will be no report,' said Strathmore firmly. 'The Society does not exist to perpetuate the memory of charlatans like Brand. I shall give you what recollections I have, however. I take the view that we have a public duty to co-operate with the police, so you may take note of anything I say and put it in your pocket-book, Sergeant. As I recall it, the first part of the evening was devoted to a table-seance and I remember handing you a piece of paper showing the disposition of the sitters.'

'I was grateful for that, sir.'

'The first indication of anything unusual was Miss Crush's observation that the temperature in the room appeared to have dropped, and that was followed by a sequence of raps on the table indicating apparently that a spirit by the name of Walter wished to get in touch. Soon after that a luminous and animated hand was observed, I believe by all present, to be present in the room, hovering above the table in front of the medium. I have no doubt that it was Brand's right hand coated with some substance of a luminous property.'

'You didn't remark upon it at the time, did you?'

'I recall that at the time I was not certain. It meant, you see, that the chain of hands was broken, and the person on his right, Miss Crush, was collaborating in a deception, which I was not prepared to accept. She is very well regarded among spiritualists. However, I have since reluctantly decided that my inference must have been correct, though I cannot imagine what caused her to betray the movement in this way.'

'What happened next, sir?'

'Miss Crush claimed to have been touched by the hand. And so did Miss Probert. She said that it was tugging at her dress. That's very odd, isn't it? You see, she was sitting on the opposite side of the table from Brand, between her fiancé and your inspector. Captain Nye objected strongly to what was going on and he was pelted with oranges for his trouble. I presume that Brand threw them. Shortly after that we put on the light.'

'Did you immediately proceed to the experiment with the chair?'

'I think we needed a few minutes to collect ourselves. I remember that I had to dissuade Probert from pouring Miss Crush a glass of gin. Nye, too, was still extremely exercised about what had happened. It was Brand who restored order eventually, by agreeing to let us sit for the second experiment in a subdued light. He was a very self-possessed young man, now that I think about him. He told Probert to show the apparatus to the rest of us. Of course, he had seen it for himself at the beginning of the evening, before everyone arrived.'

'He'd also seen it the previous evening,' Cribb reminded Strathmore.

'So he had. Well, while the rest of us were looking at the chair, Brand busied himself tidying up the oranges and flowers – a vase of chrysanthemums had been knocked over by an orange. We soon had the apparatus ready, and several of the party took turns to sit in the chair. At that stage it was working perfectly. Brand was searched and seated in the chair. We retired behind the curtain and the seance commenced. I was taking the galvanometer readings with Inspector Jowett. I remember that Miss Crush was the first to announce that she felt a supernatural presence in the room and shortly afterwards Miss Probert claimed that her hair was being stroked.'

'You all remained seated, however?' asked Cribb.

'Every one of us. You may imagine the effect upon the company of what happened next. We all heard quite distinctly the sound of footsteps from behind the curtain while the galvanometer was steady at a reading of 188!'

'What did you do, sir?'

'First there were shouts from behind the curtain, punctuated, I may say, by some strong language which we doubted at first could have been spoken by Brand. Dr Probert asked me to look behind the curtain.'

'And what did you see?'

'Nothing. The study was in darkness, without even the light from the fire that we had next door. Brand asked me to fetch Probert, and, as the doctor went into the study, he kicked over the bowl of salt solution we had used to strengthen the contact with the medium's hands. I went back to light a candle and we all went in to see what had happened. Captain Nye was sent downstairs to turn off the current.'

'I believe that Mr Brand was in quite an agitated state.'

'My word, yes. He was convinced that one of us had ventured behind the curtain, which would have been unforgiveable. The Society does not conduct itself like that, as I told you. I think it was Miss Crush who finally regained Brand's co-operation by persuading him that we may actually have had a spirit visitor with us. We later learned, of course, that it had been Professor Quayle stumbling by error into the wrong room.'

'I think he was trying to evade me at the time, sir.'

Strathmore nodded. 'I think each one of us must admit to a measure of blame for the things that happened that evening, Sergeant. Where was I? Ah yes, by the time Captain Nye came up from the cellar we were ready to resume the experiment, so the poor fellow was sent straight down again to switch the electricity on while we resumed our seats in the library.'

'Do you happen to remember who was the last person to leave the study?' asked Cribb.

'It must have been Probert. I remember him drawing the curtain.'

'And you returned to the galvanometer?'

'I did. It was twenty minutes to eleven and we had a reading of 202. The next thing I recall is the door-handle turning and you arriving in the room. It gave us quite a shock, Sergeant, I can tell you.'

'But not so big a shock as Mr Brand was getting, eh?'

said Cribb a little coarsely. 'Well, sir, you've been very helpful. I think you've covered all the matters I was wanting to ask about.'

'Possibly it helps that we are both investigators in our different ways, Sergeant,' said Strathmore, standing up. 'Without seeming to boast, I think I know what you peelers require from a witness. Might I inquire whether you have come to a conclusion yet about Brand's death?'

'I think I'm closer to it now than I was, sir. Have you formed any opinion about it yourself, by any chance?'

'Oh yes,' said Strathmore. 'I am quite certain how it happened, but I should not wish to prejudice your investigation. When you have made up your mind, you must let me know, and I shall tell you whether we have both arrived at the same conclusion.'

12

> They've had their wish – called for the naked truth,
> And in she tripped, sat down and bade them stare;
> They had to blush a little and forgive!

Pursuing Miss Probert had a beneficial effect on Thackeray. Trailing a suspect was a duty he had performed more times than he cared to remember, but suspects with trim figures and elegant deportment were rare. Trailing was not quite the word to describe his sprightly step along Hill Street. He moved like a man twenty years his junior.

The difficulty was in convincing himself that she was a suspect at all. A young woman who devoted so much of her time to distributing food to the impoverished was not his notion of a murderess, however incriminating Cribb might regard the presence of a brush and comb in her basket. A dagger or a tin of weed-killer Thackeray was ready to be impressed by, but a brush and comb? He grinned to himself as he threaded his way through the shoppers of Richmond.

By crossing the street he gave himself a longer view of the pavement Alice Probert travelled along. An additional advantage of this parallel route was that she was unlikely to suspect his presence. People always supposed that if anyone chose to follow them they would automatically use the same side of the street.

He spotted her at once, waiting to cross at the junction with Red Lion Street. A young constable on traffic duty waved two four-wheelers past before halting a cart to allow her to cross. She nodded her thanks and stepped forward. She would be easy to keep in sight, with that bar of white on the trimming of her hat. She was not paying the smallest attention to Thackeray's side of the street, but he went through the motions of making sure there were other pedestrians between himself and his quarry and occasionally altering his stride to take advantage of the cover of a passing vehicle.

Across Red Lion Street she stopped to exchange words with an older woman in a grey coat who had obviously been shopping, for an elderly manservant weighed down with parcels had stopped at the same time and stood patiently some yards behind her. It occurred to Thackeray that Alice must be well known in Richmond, at least among the well-to-do. Whatever felonies she intended with her brush and comb she was going to find it difficult to avoid being recognized. He stopped beside a tobacconist's and waited, like the man with the parcels, for the end of the conversation.

Several minutes later, she took her leave of the woman in grey and moved on towards the point where Hill Street curved to the right and became George Street. To the left was Richmond Green, to the right the Parish Church, and ahead, beyond the Quadrant, the railway station. She chose none of these directions. Instead, she opened the door of a shop on the right and went inside. Thackeray stepped briskly ahead and drew level with the shop. It was a milliner's. He though of the brush and comb and smiled broadly. Cribb had not included a hat-shop in his calculations.

The window of the shop was arranged on the principle that the more goods one displayed, the greater was the chance of engaging the attention of a customer. From Thackeray's side of the street the hats in their rows looked not too different from the arrangement of apples in the greengrocer's next door.

He prepared to wait again. Five minutes passed by the clock over the jeweller's midway along George Street. He was rather charmed by this little interlude in Alice Probert's charitable excursion. Much as he admired young women with social consciences, he liked to be assured that they occasionally slipped into a milliner's and tried on hats.

After another five minutes cold feet were beginning to occupy him more than saintly women. Nobody had gone into the shop since Alice, and one customer, dressed in brown, had emerged. The stream of traffic and pedestrians coursed past him, emphasizing how inactive he was. Then the disquieting thought came to him that there might be another entrance at the back of the shop, with access from Red Lion Street. He crossed the street in the direction of the greengrocer's and turned and walked past the milliner's, with the merest glance through the window. To his mortification there was nobody inside but a shop-assistant arranging a bonnet on a stand.

He turned about and pushed open the door. The assistant was a girl of thirteen or so. Her eyes opened wide at the arrival of an unaccompanied man in the shop. 'May I help you, sir?' she said, more as an expression of surprise than a promise of assistance.

'I hope so. I was looking for my – er – niece. I thought she came in here to try on a hat a few minutes ago.'

'You must be mistaken, sir. We haven't had a customer in here for half an hour.'

Half an hour? It had not been that long. 'I'm sure she came in,' Thackeray insisted. 'There ain't a back door to the shop, is there?'

'No, sir. Perhaps if you could tell me how madam was dressed . . .'

'Dark green coat,' said Thackeray. He was good at descriptions. 'Hat the same colour, trimmed with white. And she was carrying a basket of oranges.'

'Oh!' said the girl, as if the clouds had rolled away. 'Wait a moment.' She crossed to a chest of drawers and took out a large purple hat. 'Was madam's hat in this style, but green in colour?'

'That's the one!' said Thackeray.

'She got it here last week,' said the girl. 'It matched her coat beautifully. But she came in fifteen minutes ago to visit Miss Barkway, the manageress. She comes almost every day. She is not a customer, sir. She is a personal friend of Miss Barkway. You *are* related to her, sir?'

'I'm her Uncle Edward,' said Thackeray at once. 'Where is she now? Through there?' He pointed to a door he had noticed behind a full-length mirror.

'That leads upstairs to Miss Barkway's rooms,' said the girl in a whisper. 'The lady always goes straight upstairs and comes down after five minutes in different clothes. I really don't know why. Perhaps you do. She left the shop a few minutes before you came in. Didn't you notice her? But of course you wouldn't if you expected to see her in the green hat. She was wearing brown. And she always covers her face with a veil.'

'Oh glory!' said Thackeray, remembering the figure he had seen come out of the shop. 'Did you by any chance notice which way she went?'

'I can't say I was watching her today, but I've sometimes seen her cross the street and go through Golden Court towards Richmond Green. It's a little paved passage—'

'I'm obliged to you, miss,' he said, already opening the door. He put his hand in his pocket and found sixpence, 'I can trust you not to say anything about this to Miss Barkway, can't I?'

Golden Court was lined with small, interesting shops where people lingered and reflected, indifferent to the activity of George Street. Thackeray's arrival on the scene, running, was met with looks of the sort traction-engines receive when they pass through small villages. Concerned only with the possibility that Alice had given him the slip, he clattered heavy-footed through the passage. Richmond Green opened to him at the end, some ten acres of turf bordered by a narrow road, with elegant houses beyond. A hundred yards ahead was the figure of a woman in brown carrying a basket. As he watched, she turned left and entered one of the buildings fronting the Green.

For an instant before he started after her, Thackeray sensed that someone else was coming after him through Golden Court. It was no more than a fleeting impression and at this moment it mattered to him less than the necessity of fixing in his mind which house Alice Probert had entered. He did not look behind him. Instead he crossed the Green to the three-storeyed terrace Alice had entered. It was an example of the period when terraces were built as gentlemen's residences rather than workmen's cottages. Indeed, as he approached the tall gate of the end house she had gone into, and looked through the wrought-iron work at the Roman pilasters and frieze that framed the front door, and at the five bays on each of the upper floors, he felt bound to ask himself what the poor of Richmond were doing behind such an exterior. And why Alice Probert chose to clothe herself in brown and wear a veil before she visited there.

He reckoned a minute had passed since she had gone inside, but there was no movement behind the ground-floor windows. He waited another two minutes, as if admiring the lines of the building, as people must often have done, and then moved on. It seemed likely that Alice was being received in a room at the rear of the house, and he wanted to confirm the fact. There was no tradesmen's entrance at the side, so he continued a few yards along the pavement until he came to a red-brick arch, which a board informed him had been the gateway to the long-demolished Richmond Palace. He went through into Old Palace Yard, turning left at a building named The Trumpeter's House. A short way ahead he recognized the rear of the terrace, surrounded by a tall brick wall. He located an unlocked gate, and entered the garden. There was a small shed to his left, close to the house, a woodstore, he decided, and a suitable place to shelter inside briefly. It did house wood, but in the form of picture-frames, several stacked against the wall and another half-constructed, supported on a carpenter's bench. An oil-painting lay nearby, presumably after being measured for its frame. It was a still life of two vegetable marrows.

He sat on the edge of the bench and considered what to do next. He had no authority to enter the house. He discounted the idea of speaking to the servants. It was safer to work alone, from outside. He would begin by making discreet observations through the windows.

He crept from the hut with a stealth that would not have disgraced a Red Indian and flitted from window to window at the rear of the house. Discouragingly, this bold manoeuvre yielded no return. The first windows he reached were so coated with condensation that the room behind could only be the kitchen, and the rest were shuttered. If he wanted to persist with the investigation he would need to raise himself by some means to the level of the first floor. He looked round for a ladder. None was available. But it is difficult to keep a Scotland Yard man down when he is determined to go up. Adjoining the back of the house was a concrete path and between the path and a small lawn was a wooden trellis supporting a Virginia creeper.

He stepped back and estimated the height of the first-floor window nearest the trellis. It was some fourteen feet above the ground. He examined the trellis. It was formed in six-inch squares. He counted twenty squares from the ground to the top. As a structure it was sturdy enough to support a Virginia creeper, but would it take a climber of fifteen stone?

He walked round to the side facing the lawn and gripped two of the upright laths and set his right boot on the lowest crosspiece and gently transferred the weight of his body from the ground to the trellis. It held, so he slotted his left boot into the space above and began a slow ascent. He would not have been surprised at any stage to hear the rending of wood, but happily for the cause of law and order he reached the top without incident.

The most difficult part was still to come. The window-sill was between three and four feet higher than the last crosspiece of the trellis. He would be obliged to raise himself above the level of the structure without any other support, and since it was set back a yard or so from the house it would be inviting disaster to reach out for the sill.

He considered the possibility of sitting astride the trellis and attempting to stand up, but he foresaw a problem in securing an adequate foothold. It was slightly less hazardous, he decided, to remain facing the house, lodge both feet on the fourth crosspiece from the top and, by straightening his body and pressing his knees against the topmost lath, achieve an upright stance. This he tried, gripping the top of the trellis with his hands until he felt sufficiently secure to let go and raise himself for a glimpse through the window.

It was only a glimpse, but there was something to see this time. The moment when he became perpendicular coincided with a rare shaft of November sunlight, and he was given a highlighted view of the back of a man in shirt-sleeves, standing close to the window putting up an artist's easel. It made him remember the frames in the shed below, and the still-life painting of marrows. In this fleeting first look, he had time for no more than an impression of the rest of the room. The sun caught the curved edge of a white globe at the other end. He concluded that it was the porcelain shade of a table lamp. He lowered himself and gripped the top of the trellis again.

After a suitable pause he rose for a second look. In those few seconds, the sun had gone in, so the surfaces it caught were less sharply defined, but because the light was more diffused and the shadows less pronounced, it was actually possible to see more of the interior. Thackeray therefore looked past the artist to see what his subject was, and his eyes returned to the white globe. He now saw that it was not what he had supposed. Unless his unusual position was producing symptoms of vertigo, there was not one white surface, spherical in shape, but two, adjacent to each other. They were not porcelain globes, nor were they part of a paraffin lamp. They were part of Miss Alice Probert, and she was standing quite still on a kind of pedestal, or podium. She was wearing no clothes at all.

For a moment after this discovery, Thackeray teetered at the top of the trellis, his equilibrium dreadfully imperilled. By shooting out his arms and using them like a tightrope walker, he succeeded in recovering sufficiently to carry out the drill every constable learns at the start of his career: that facts must always be checked. He looked through the window for the third time.

There was no disputing the fact that there was a man at an easel in the room or that a young woman was posing naked in front of him. It is difficult, of course, positively to identify somebody in a state of nature whom you have met clothed for the first time the same morning, but Thackeray was as certain as he could be that he was looking at Alice Probert. True, she was in half-profile, or rather her face was (he was trying to ignore the rest of her, which apart from general indications as to stature was more distracting than helpful to the process of identification), and her black hair had been unpinned and allowed to lie loosely over her shoulders, but her piercing blue eyes (mercifully focused on the wall), the slight pertness of her nose and cheek-bones and the way she held her head were conclusive in his opinion. Having done all that duty required, Thackeray relaxed his knees and resumed his handhold on the trellis. This was fortunate, because he was immediately subject to a second shock, a voice from below him in the garden.

'If you have quite finished up there, I'll trouble you to come down here and explain what you are doing.' It was a young man's voice and it carried authority and, unless Thackeray was mistaken, intimations of hostility.

He looked down, but was unable to recognize the speaker through the Virginia creeper, which had been comprehensively disarranged in the last minutes. He decided it was probably safest to give an account of himself on *terra firma*, so he clambered down as swiftly as the plant would permit him.

His discoverer was young, as he had supposed, certainly not more than twenty-five, and tall. He was wearing a ulster and billycock. His face was unusually long in shape, dominated by a large mouth, and teeth which looked as though they would not fit into the space available. Thackeray could not decide which member of the animal kingdom he was reminded of, except that it was not domestic.

'Before you fabricate a story,' said the young man, 'I think I should inform you that I have been observing your movements for some considerable time, and it is useless to deny that you have been following Miss Probert about Richmond for the past three-quarters of an hour. I don't know who you are, sir, or what your game is, but I'll have you know that nobody is going to do that sort of thing without answering to me.'

'Perhaps you'll tell me who you are, then,' said Thackeray.

'Certainly. I am Captain Nye, Miss Probert's fiancé.'

'I see. My name is Thackeray. It won't mean much to you, sir.'

'You're damned right about that, Thackeray. The only things I know about you, I don't like, and I demand an account of them. I don't know what Richmond's coming to when a young lady can't move about without being pursued by a shabbily-dressed man old enough to be her father.'

'I'd be obliged if you would leave my clothes out of this,' said Thackeray, mustering what dignity he could. He was uncertain what he ought to say to Nye about his purpose in trailing Alice, but he was quite sure it would be a mistake to tell the whole truth, and he needed time to discover what would satisfy the captain. Best, in the circumstances, to keep him talking. 'Are you worried that I might have designs on your fiancée, then?'

'You're damned impertinent, sir!' said Nye. 'I ought to hand you over to the police. It might surprise you to know that the gentleman escorting Miss Probert down Richmond Hill this morning, when you were following them, was a detective-sergeant from Scotland Yard.'

'My word!' said Thackeray.

'I don't know what you said when you approached them by the Bridge. I suppose it was some form of begging. The sergeant very decently bought you some chestnuts, I noticed, but what sort of gratitude did you show? No sooner had the fellow got on a bus than you were away in pursuit of Miss Probert.'

'The chestnuts was my reward for carrying her basket down the hill,' said Thackeray.

'That was your excuse, was it? A pity she didn't see through you straight away. Unfortunately, my fiancée is one of the most generous-hearted girls alive. The basket you carried undoubtedly contained comestibles for the poor and needy. She devotes her life to charitable enterprises. I hope that makes you feel ashamed of your behaviour, sir.'

'I was only looking at her,' said Thackeray.

'Oh, yes, I know the sort of thing men like you get up to. It's quite harmless, you say, simply enjoying the sight of a pretty woman. Soon enough, you're not just watching them walk by, you're following them, and the next step is what I've caught you in the act of doing – peering through windows.'

'I wanted to be sure it was Miss Probert,' said Thackeray truthfully. 'She went into the hat-shop and I was taken by surprise when she came out with a different set of clothes.'

'Is it surprising?' said Nye. 'She visits some very seedy areas in her work. She can't go into places like that dressed in plush hats and velvet coats, by Jove. They'd tear 'em off her back in parts of Twickenham.'

'Why doesn't she put on her brown clothes from the beginning then?'

'There's no mystery in it. She's the daughter of a doctor. The Proberts are a well-known family on the Hill. People expect them to dress decently. That's all there is to it. Look here, I'm damned if I'm going to account for everything to you. I want to know what you were doing at the top of that trellis.'

'I was trying to look into that window,' admitted Thackeray.

'You were, eh?' Nye came a step closer to Thackeray. 'What did you expect to see?'

'Not what was there, anyway.'

'I'm damned sure of that,' said Nye. 'You're a shameless brute, aren't you? A Peeping Tom. See if this will close your nasty little eye!' His clenched fist landed squarely in

Thackeray's face, with such speed and force that it toppled him over on to the lawn. 'It may interest you to know,' Nye went on, massaging his knuckles, 'that this house is a meeting place of the Philanthropic Ladies of Richmond, and my fiancée comes here regularly. You'll see nothing to your obnoxious taste at any of the windows here, by Jove! But if I ever find you within half a mile of that innocent girl, that sweet champion of the unfortunate, I'll thrash you within an inch of your life!'

When Thackeray got up, Nye had already gone. He patted the skin round his eye with his fingertips. There was no bleeding, but he was going to have a black eye that would want some explaining at Paradise Street, and only for trying to do his duty. There was no justice in it.

He let himself out of the gate and walked through the courtyard and back past the terrace. At the last house his attention was taken by a small board attached to the railings. The name of the terrace was Maids of Honour Row.

13

I've been so happy with you! Nice stuffed chairs,
And sympathetic sideboards; what an end
To all the instructive evenings!

'She was as naked as the day she was born.'

'So you've told me, Thackeray, twice already,' said Cribb unappreciatively. 'I understood what you said the first time.'

'But hang it all, Sarge, you haven't said so much as a blimey. A young lady like Miss Probert don't stand in front of an artist without a stitch on every day of the week.'

'On the contrary,' said Cribb. 'I wouldn't be surprised if she *does*. Pictures don't get painted at a single sitting. Your modern artist believes in fidelity to nature, and that means every eyelash.'

'Well, it ain't seemly, according to my notion of things,' responded Thackeray, who was not easily put down.

'According to some notions it ain't seemly for a member of the Force to be looking into a first-floor window from the top of a trellis,' Cribb uncharitably pointed out. 'How's the eye? I've seen some shiners in my time, but this one beats 'em all.'

It was the morning after the episode in Maids of Honour

Row, and they were in Richmond again, at that moment mounting the steps of the police station. 'I'd be obliged if you wouldn't bring up the subject of Miss Probert again, Constable,' said Cribb, 'particularly in the company in here this morning. If I ask you to confirm anything, simply nod your head. Well, you can say "yes" if you like, but I want no more talk of artists or undressing, and that's an order.'

'Yes, Sergeant.'

A room had been assigned to Cribb for the morning. In the corner waiting, sitting perfectly still under a hatstand – a serviceable substitute for a potted palm – was Mrs Probert.

'Ah, you got my message, then, ma'am,' said Cribb.

She answered without turning her face. 'I should not be here otherwise, Sergeant. You gave me to understand that I might be able to speak with—'

'It is all arranged, ma'am. But tell me first: the proposal in my letter regarding tomorrow night – is that in order?'

'Is it likely that I would refuse? As I told you on a previous occasion, I have a horror of seances and I shall remain in my room, but if you believe that reconstructing the events of last Saturday will assist your investigation, the house is at your disposal. You will tell my husband, of course?'

'That will be taken care of,' Cribb promised. 'Now, the other matter. As you know, we are holding a certain party in custody in this building, and I have made arrangements for him to be brought up presently from the cells.'

'This is very accommodating of you.'

'Not at all, ma'am. I have my reasons. But before we bring the professor in, I should like to explain a little matter of police procedure. As you know, we detained him – or rather, you did, with your book of sermons – on Saturday night. I charged him under what is known as the Larceny Act of 1861, with entering a dwelling-house in the night with intent to commit a felony therein. He also admitted to certain other offences, namely removing a vase from Miss Crush's possession and a painting from your husband's, but I have not charged him with these. It's not necessary, if you follow me, to bring more than one charge at a time.'

'I think my husband would prefer it if the charges were not brought at all,' said Mrs Probert. 'He is inclined to be unsocial about his collection of pictures.'

'Understandably, ma'am. I believe Miss Crush is not enthusiastic about pressing the charges either. Of course I should not take any account of that if I regarded Professor Quayle as a danger to the public.'

'He certainly isn't that,' said Mrs Probert firmly.

'I'm glad to hear you say it, ma'am, because I value your opinion. I believe it's right to say that you have known the professor for some considerable time.'

A change came over Mrs Probert's face, as if Cribb had peeled away a mask. She blinked, her brow furrowed and she actually turned towards him. 'Who told you that?'

'That's confidential, ma'am, but I have it on good authority that the professor has visited the house quite regular. He used to bring sweets for your daughter when she was small.'

'Yes, yes. That is correct,' said Mrs Probert quickly. 'He is a harmless man. He is no more wicked than you or your assistant.'

'Thank you, ma'am. But I hope you understand my problem. Even if I set aside the matters of the vase and picture, I'm left with the original charge, and if the professor is convicted there's a minimum sentence of three years' penal servitude for that.'

'Three years – how dreadful!'

'And a maximum of seven,' added Cribb for completeness. 'It did cross my mind, though, that if the professor wanted to commit a felony that night he would have done better to have broken into an empty house, such as Miss Crush's. I posted Thackeray in Eaton Square for that very reason, didn't I, Constable?'

'Yes,' said Thackeray, remembering the injunction to answer in monosyllables.

'But there's no denying that he came to Richmond,' Cribb continued. 'I followed him to your house myself, and saw him go inside. He pushed open the back door. Now that's one of several curious things about that night. The door wasn't locked. He pushed it open just as if he was expecting it to be unlocked. He wasn't even carrying any of the tools a housebreaker uses. He had nothing more incriminating upon him than a flask of gin. I like a drop of gin occasional myself, ma'am. Do you?'

'I'm not sure what you intend by that question,' said Mrs Probert slowly.

'Just this, ma'am.' Cribb picked up a chair, planted it a yard from Mrs Probert and sat down. 'If I could be certain that Professor Quayle entered your house for a reason that the law would not describe as a felony, I could drop the charge. He could walk out of here this morning a free man.'

Mrs Probert had taken out a handkerchief and was twisting it between the fingers of her left hand. Her knuckles were white.

'If it was a confidential reason,' Cribb went on, 'nothing

need be repeated outside this room. I'm the soul of discretion myself and Thackeray over there would forget his own name if I asked him to.'

She shook her head. 'I never confide in people. It's not the way we behave in our family.'

'Your family isn't here, ma'am,' Cribb reasonably pointed out. 'It's Professor Quayle we're thinking of. Three years – that's the devil of a long time for a man as sensitive as he is.'

The lace along one edge of the handkerchief tore between Mrs Probert's fingers. She crumpled it quickly in her hand.

'Let's see,' Cribb airily continued. 'If he's convicted in Surrey, he'll have to spend it in Wandsworth, some of it with hard labour, I shouldn't be surprised. Do you know what that means, Mrs Probert?'

She drew a deep breath. 'You have done this before, haven't you? You know exactly how to phrase your questions to cause the greatest possible distress. You are not a gentleman.'

If she was trying to injure her interrogator in return, it was not successful. 'I wasn't brought up to be one, ma'am. Nor are the warders I know in Wandsworth jail.'

She closed her eyes tight for several seconds, as if to shut out the image Cribb was seeking to implant in her mind.

'Can't say I've ever seen a convict I would call a gent,' Cribb went on, 'but I suppose some must have *started* that way. After three months' hard, you wouldn't know the difference. They talk the same and they even look the same. It must be the skilly they feed them – it's a wonderful leveller is skilly.'

Mrs Probert opened her eyes and resumed her sphinx-like gaze across the room, as if that would afford some relief from the pain of what she was to say. 'Yes, I know what prison would do to him. It would break him in mind and body, and, as you rightly calculate, no woman's secret is worth such a price. I shall tell you what happened for his sake, and I hope and pray that there is some compassion in you. The professor came to our house on Saturday night at my invitation. He came to visit me in my room. I knew that my husband would be fully occupied downstairs. I left the back door unbolted. Professor Quayle is, as you have discovered, an old friend. If I tell you that our occasional evenings together were innocent in everything but the sharing of a small bottle of gin, I know that you have every right to disbelieve me, as my husband unquestionably will when he hears of this.'

Cribb shook his head. 'In this investigation, ma'am, I've heard no end of things I disbelieved, but I've no reason yet to doubt anything I've heard from you, and that includes the statement you have just made. As for your husband, I can think of no way he would get to hear about these meetings, can you, Thackeray?'

'No.' Thackeray threw caution to the winds and added, 'Definitely not, Sergeant.'

'Fetch the professor, then, and have the darbies taken off him first.' When Thackeray had left on this errand, Cribb confided to Mrs Probert, 'He's totally reliable. Got his black eye for safeguarding a lady's secret.'

The reunion of the professor and Mrs Probert was simple and affecting, the more so considering that she had knocked him insensible at their last meeting. He entered the room, white, gaunt, with clothes creased and chin unshaven, and crossed to where she was under the hatstand and took her hands.

'Winifred!'

'Eustace!'

'Your flask of gin is with the duty sergeant at the desk outside, sir,' said Cribb, as a sort of benediction. 'I offer my apologies for the inconvenience you've been put to since Saturday night. You understand that we only became aware of the facts this morning. Mrs Probert has made it clear that your purpose in entering her dwelling-house was not felonious.'

An affectionate look passed between the professor and Mrs Probert before he told Cribb, 'You did no more than your duty, Sergeant.'

'Thank you, sir. Before you leave, however, I wonder if you'd oblige me by clarifying one small point.'

'Naturally, if I can.'

'It concerns a certain hat-shop not far from here, and the visits Miss Alice Probert makes there.'

The professor glanced nervously at Mrs Probert, who was the first to respond. 'What is the professor presumed to know about my daughter and a hat-shop, Sergeant?'

'That she often visits there, ma'am. I didn't put the point to you because it was unnecessary. On my first call at your house, you passed a remark about it. If you remember, your husband explained your daughter's absence by saying that she was on a charitable excursion and you commented that she was buying a hat.'

'So I did,' agreed Mrs Probert.

'A small matter, really, or so it seemed at the time,' continued Cribb. 'There was young Alice going off with an armful of marrows to do good works, and on the way she was slipping into a milliner's to try on hats. Nothing criminal in it. Just something to smile over. I suppose a friend of yours must have told you that Alice is in the habit of going in there, or was it one of the servants?'

'It was Hitchman,' Mrs Probert confirmed.

'The deaf woman? Sharp eyes, that one, and not above telling a tale about the young lady of the house. I don't suppose the information troubled you, or you wouldn't have mentioned it to the professor. It was just a joke, and you passed it on to an old friend, didn't you?'

Mrs Probert nodded.

'And you, sir,' Cribb went on, turning to Quayle, 'mentioned it to your young lodger, Peter Brand, in the way people pass on an amusing story.'

'I must confess that I did,' the professor agreed.

'But then the story came back to you and your husband, ma'am,' said Cribb. 'Peter Brand came to your house on the night before the seance and repeated it, with one significant addition. He had taken the trouble to follow Alice to the shop one morning and had seen her go inside and come out ten minutes later, veiled and dressed in different clothes. What construction could you put upon it but that she was secretly visiting somebody? That was certainly Brand's interpretation, and it was sufficient to secure your husband's co-operation during the seance.'

'Co-operation?' said Mrs Probert. 'What do you mean by that?'

'You must understand that Brand was a sharp – a confidence trickster, ma'am. He found that calling up the spirits in Richmond and Belgravia was a better game by far than working a pea and thimbles on a sordid little fairground. He needed help, of course. Even your thimble-rigger has his nobblers in the crowd around him. He secured accomplices by blackmailing 'em. The price of his silence was not money, but collaboration. He needed your husband's help, so he found a way to blackmail him, and he very shrewdly judged that the best lever he had on Dr Probert was not his own reputation, but his daughter's.'

'The monster!' said Quayle.

'I have always known she would be the ruin of us,' said Mrs Probert, leaving no doubt whom she regarded as the monster. 'That girl never gives a thought to the consequences of her behaviour.'

Cribb treated the comment as Dr Probert would have done: he ignored it. 'He was just a clever sharp, sir. I wouldn't put it any stronger than that.'

'Well, I would, Sergeant,' Quayle insisted. 'Damn it, he was impugning Miss Probert's reputation, and the unfortunate young lady didn't know a thing about it.'

'I rather think she did, sir,' said Cribb. 'If you had studied the circumstances of the seance, as I have, you would know that Miss Alice herself made some extraordinary claims. At one point in the evening she announced that a spirit hand was pulling at her dress, and later that her hair was being stroked. I believe that Brand had made a separate approach to Alice and told her what he had seen when he followed her. He threatened to tell everything to Captain Nye unless she agreed to assist him in producing fraudulent effects.'

'Are you saying that he was blackmailing Dr Probert and his daughter at the same time, and with the same information?'

'Yes, sir. He was a clever sharp, as I said. Neither of 'em was to know that the other was being blackmailed, of course. And if you think *that* was cool, consider the fact that it was

190

all based upon a supposition – that because Miss Alice changed her clothes at the milliner's, she was visiting a lover, begging your pardon, ma'am.'

'*She* is the one who should beg your pardon,' said Mrs Probert.

'A supposition, you say,' said Quayle. 'Do you have any reason to think she was not on her way to an assignation?'

'In point of fact, I do, sir,' Cribb answered. 'Miss Probert went out on one of her little jaunts yesterday morning, and I ordered Constable Thackeray to follow her and observe discreetly what went on.'

'My word! And did you, Constable?'

Thackeray went a shade pinker. 'Yes, sir.'

'Really? Well, do not keep us in suspense. What was she really doing?'

Thackeray was never more relieved to hear Cribb clear his throat prior to speaking. 'Before we go into that, sir, I think we might ask Mrs Probert the same question. I'm sure that as Miss Alice was allowed to visit the hat-shop yesterday, she must have given a satisfactory explanation to her parents.'

Everyone looked at Mrs Probert, who continued to look at the wall in front of her. 'Her father spoke to her, yes. Something had to be said, although it is difficult in our family. He dotes on her, but we have lost the facility for natural conversation. After Peter Brand had died, however, it was important to show the girl what an impossible situation she had put her father in by her inconsiderate behaviour, so he spoke to her on Sunday over the main course at dinner. It was roast lamb. She succeeded in convincing us that she has no secret lover. She is still devoted to Captain Nye.'

'Capital news!' exclaimed Professor Quayle.

'The captain, too, is quite enslaved,' continued Mrs Probert, with no more enthusiasm than if she was reading from a newspaper. 'As it transpires, his infatuation is the clue to Alice's eccentric conduct. You may have noticed that William is a possessive, not to say jealous, young man where my daughter is concerned. He has lately taken to following her about. She pretended not to notice, and at first it was quite flattering to her, but soon it started to be inconvenient. A young lady likes to be looked at by her admirer, but that is not the same as being under permanent surveillance. She could not go anywhere without feeling she was being overlooked. She decided to resort to subterfuge. She arranged with a friend who owns the milliner's in George Street that she would go in there and change her clothes when she wanted to escape from the unrelenting vigilance. That was the explanation she gave. It may seem unfair, but my daughter thinks that William's conduct is a little unfair, too. She has an independent turn of mind.'

'I've discovered that, ma'am,' said Cribb.

'She explained that her little subterfuge enables her to take a stand for liberty.'

'So it does, ma'am. So it does,' said Cribb. 'Thackeray, you observed Miss Probert yesterday. Wouldn't you agree that she has taken a stand for liberty?'

'Yes, Sergeant.' Thackeray blushed again, but Mrs Probert did not turn her eyes in his direction.

After they had gone, Thackeray took quick advantage of the restoration of free speech. 'They don't know about Miss Probert's posing, Sarge! She hasn't told them.'

'Did you really think she would?' asked Cribb. 'If she

had, I'm sure Dr Probert wouldn't have allowed her to go to Maids of Honour Row yesterday morning. No, she satisfied them that she isn't visiting a lover, and that was what they wanted to hear. I had doubts about the excursions myself when I saw the brush and comb in her basket. It was quite a reassurance to learn from you that it was all in the cause of Fine Art.'

'But she's taking a terrible risk by continuing to do it.'

'I expect the painting isn't finished yet,' said Cribb matter-of-factly.

Thackeray's face was a study. 'How ever could a young lady as decently brought up as Miss Probert, with all her advantages, bring herself to do such a thing?'

'Oh, it ain't so remarkable if you know a thing or two about human nature,' said Cribb. 'I shouldn't think a young girl would get much attention in that family, would you? It's well-known that girls often idolize their fathers – how else can they get to understand the opposite sex – and they only ask a modicum of affection in return. But how much notice did Alice get from Dr Probert? He was too devoted to the nymphs disporting themselves round the walls of his gallery to take any notice of his daughter or his wife. So it's logical that she should behave as she did; he had shown her only one way to win a man's admiration.'

'You make it sound quite sensible, Sarge,' admitted Thackeray, who had never previously considered Cribb as an authority on the upbringing of girls. 'The odd thing is that in spite of everything she seems to have won the admiration of Captain Nye.'

'Hm. He'll take some understanding,' said Cribb, almost to himself. 'Well, Thackeray, it's time we reported to Inspector Jowett. Got to lay our plans for tomorrow night.'

193

'Did I understand correct, Sarge? Are you going to recon-struct the seance at the Proberts' house?'

'Quite correct,' said Cribb. It's all arranged. Everyone has promised to be there. I shall want your help as well.'

'Certainly, Sarge. But what are we trying to achieve?'

'An arrest.'

'Jerusalem! As soon as this?'

'As soon as this my foot! We've been through all the evidence and talked to all the suspects. It's just a matter now of showing how the thing was done and clapping the darbies on the murderer. I'd make an arrest today, but I think if we leave it till tomorrow we might get a confession.'

'I'm sure I don't know who's going to confess,' said Thackeray in a tone indicating that Cribb might have had the decency to keep his assistant fully informed. 'It isn't one of those two we've just been talking to, is it? Mrs Probert had a strong dislike for Peter Brand and his spiritualism.'

'That may be so,' said Cribb, 'but she wouldn't arrange for a visit from Professor Quayle on the night she was planning to commit a murder. And I can't believe that Quayle would have gone upstairs if he had murdered Brand; he would have left the house at once, in hopes that nobody had seen him. No, the act of murder had to be committed by one of the six people participating in the seance, as I shall demonstrate tomorrow evening.'

'Six?' There was a pause while Thackeray made a mental calculation. 'Miss Crush, Dr Probert, Miss Alice Probert, Mr Strathmore, Captain Nye. Who else is there?'

'Inspector Jowett.'

Thackeray grinned. 'Haven't you been able to eliminate him, Sarge?'

'Not yet. I must admit there have been times . . .'

'I think he's indestructible,' said Thackeray, and when Cribb's features promised to crease into the start of a smile he added, 'Sarge, I'm still not completely clear how the murder was done.'

'You're not?' said Cribb blankly.

'If you know who done it, you must be certain *how* it was done,' Thackeray persisted.

'But I've been over all the evidence with you,' said Cribb.

'I appreciate that, Sarge, but I'd appreciate it more if you would tell me which piece of evidence told you how the medium was killed.'

'The list of objects found on his body,' said Cribb.

'His personal possessions. I can remember them,' said Thackeray. 'There was a watch, a railway ticket, a box of matches, a cigarette case, a key-ring, a wallet and some money.'

'Well done,' said Cribb.

'The answer's among that lot, is it?' said Thackeray.

'No it ain't,' said Cribb. 'That's the whole crux of it. It ought to be, and it ain't.'

14

'Manifestations are so weak at first!
Doubting, moreover, kills them, cuts all short,
Cures with a vengeance!'

There was not much conversation being exchanged across the table in Dr Probert's library, although every one of the original sitters had arrived, with the understandable exception of the late Peter Brand, whose place was taken by Sergeant Cribb. In keeping with rank, however, it was Inspector Jowett who called the gathering to order. The tension did not ease, but it now had a focus.

'Ladies and gentlemen,' said Jowett, 'the circumstances of this evening's gathering are unusual to say the least, and none of us can feel particularly comfortable at this moment. I do assure you that I should not have inflicted such an experience upon you unless it were necessary to the investigation of Mr Brand's death.'

'His happy release,' interjected Miss Crush, who was dressed in black bombazine.

'I beg your pardon, madam.'

'In the movement we do not speak of death, Inspector. If you like you may say that he has joined the choir invisible.'

'As you please, madam. The point I wish to convey is

that Scotland Yard is grateful for the co-operation of you all. Before we turn out the light I must ask you to behave exactly as you did on Saturday evening. Some of you – let us be perfectly candid with each other – assisted the medium in producing phenomena. I shall not go into the reasons for this; I simply appeal to you in the name of law and order to play your part in precisely re-creating the events of that seance.'

'But how can we, without the medium?' asked Alice.

'Sergeant Cribb will play the part of the late Mr Brand,' Jowett explained. 'I have given him a full account of what happened.'

'He is a sensitive,' Miss Crush confided to the others in a stage whisper.

'Shall we begin?' said Jowett. 'I believe you turned out the light, Doctor.'

Before the switch was turned, Cribb glanced rapidly round the table at the faces of the fellow-sitters: Miss Crush, on his right, eyes agape with expectation; Strathmore, by contrast grimly sceptical, even his monocle flashing hostility; Jowett with the fixed smile of a chairman anticipating trouble; Alice, dignified, demure and difficult to connect with Maids of Honour Row; Captain Nye, head erect as if in the front line of battle (and the Soudan campaign suggested itself here, for as Probert had once remarked, there was a striking resemblance to the features of a camel); and finally Probert himself, on his feet to switch off the light, red-faced and frowning, but visibly deflated since Saturday.

The light went out.

'Kindly link hands,' said Jowett, sounding oddly like a dancing-instructor.

197

'Surely it isn't necessary to re-enact last Saturday so slavishly as that?' protested Nye. 'Holding hands in these conditions is a very doubtful practice, and I objected to it then. My fiancée is not used to being grasped by strange men.'

'But William, you are holding my right hand and the inspector has my left,' said Alice.

'You agreed to co-operate,' Jowett reminded him.

'Only after somebody approached my Commanding Officer. Very well, but tell me the moment anything untoward occurs, Alice.'

Cribb smiled in the darkness, imagining how Jowett would receive that remark, but no more was said on the matter. It was time, anyway, to begin his own part in the proceedings. He moved forward in his chair and turned his feet on their sides to bring the heels of his boots silently into contact, face to face. Then he addressed the company: 'I believe Mr Brand began by asking you not to be alarmed if anybody behaved irregular. I make the same request, ladies and gentlemen. Soon after this one of you indicated that you sensed a supernatural presence in the room.' As a cue, he gently squeezed Miss Crush's left hand.

'Oh! It's me!' she announced in a squeak. 'That is to say, I did.'

'Say it again then, madam,' said Jowett with an obvious effort to be amiable.

'I sense a presence,' said Miss Crush flatly.

'Is anyone trying to get in touch?' asked Cribb with rather more conviction. The whole situation verged on the ridiculous and it was only too easy to imagine what they would make of it in the mess-room at the Yard, but having brought himself to the brink, so to speak, he was not the man to stand quivering there.

'Not a thing,' said Nye, after some five seconds had passed. 'The whole exercise is futile, in my opinion.'

'Is there anyone there?' asked Cribb. He pressed the soles of his shoes together and gently clicked his heels three times.

'Did you hear that?' demanded Miss Crush.

Before anyone had time to respond there were five independent raps. They appeared to have originated from Alice's area of the table.

'Alphabet,' said Dr Probert mechanically.

'There is no need for that,' said Miss Crush. 'We know it will be Uncle Walter.'

Cribb clicked three times to confirm the fact and at the same time withdrew his right hand from Miss Crush's grasp. She passed no comment. By keeping two of his fingers folded against his palm he had avoided rubbing off much of the fluor-spar he had assiduously applied before the seance. The hand was warm from being held in front of the fire a few minutes before.

'I recollect that we were treated to the apparent manifestation of a spirit hand at this juncture,' said Strathmore in a bored voice which changed dramatically to exclaim, 'My eyes! There it is!'

Perhaps because he had not had the opportunity of seeing Brand's performance, Cribb's hand-movements were different in character, more suggestive of traffic-control duty than the conducting of the choir invisible, but the fluor-spar glowed bravely, drawing gasps of admiration.

'How the devil did that thing get in here?' asked Nye. 'We want no repetition of that deplorable episode last time.'

'You can't stop it!' cried Miss Crush excitedly. 'I can feel my skirt being pulled already.'

'Mine too,' said Alice, adding quickly, 'It is lightly fingering the hem, William, that is all.'

The pace of events surprised even Cribb. An orange thudded against Captain Nye before he had a chance to protest about the skirt-pulling. Cribb noticed that Dr Probert was no longer holding his left hand. Another orange bounced across the table. A bellow from Nye signalled a second hit.

'I say!' called Strathmore. 'This is carrying verisimilitude too far!'

'Lights, if you please,' said Cribb.

Dr Probert obliged by going to the switch, but not before another orange had found its mark. When the lights went on, Nye was seen to be stooping below the level of the table.

'My poor William!' said Alice, leaning over to stroke his forehead, on which a red mark was forming. 'You must be bruised all over.'

'I'd like to know who was so beastly inconsiderate as to set out another bowl of oranges,' muttered Nye.

'They were there on my instruction,' said Jowett. 'Most obliging of you to take a second pummelling so manfully, Captain. The East Surreys can be proud of you. Now, ladies and gentlemen, I think we have reproduced the first half of the seance with passable fidelity, with one small exception which we must not overlook.' He got up from the table and approached the mantelpiece behind Nye's chair. 'I recollect that on Saturday this vase of chrysanthemums was tipped over by a stray orange, like so.' He pushed his forefinger towards the vase and gently toppled it on to its side. The water coursed along the shelf and dropped noisily into the hearth.

'That's mahogany, damn you!' said Probert, starting towards it.

'It won't hurt if it is kept well polished,' said Jowett, waving him back. 'If I have it right, the medium wiped the surface dry with his handkerchief while the rest of us examined the chair in the study.' He beckoned to Cribb with his finger. 'If you please, Sergeant.'

Cribb set to work with a white handkerchief he had thoughtfully brought with him, and the others obediently followed Jowett through the curtain into the study. By the time the call came for Cribb to take his place in the chair, he had mopped up the water, removed the fluor-spar from his hand and drawn aside the fire-screen.

He went through to the study. Probert and Strathmore were ready with lint and salted water. It reminded him rather of visiting the dentist, except that in this surgery six attendants surrounded the chair and one of them was a murderer.

Probert dipped two small squares of lint into the water and placed them over the brass handles attached to the arms of the chair. 'Please sit down, Sergeant, and grip the handles. Captain Nye, would you be so good as to go down to the cellar and switch off the electric power until I call out to you to turn it on again? Alice, would you light the candles, please?'

In a matter of minutes the chair was ready and a gentle current was passing through Cribb and registering 200 divisions on the galvanometer.

Everyone but Cribb returned to the other side of the curtain and the candles were extinguished. The play of firelight on the faces of the sitters caught clear indication of apprehension that had not been evident before. However artificial the reconstruction had been so far, it was fast approaching the moment when its purpose was inescapably relevant.

'Do you have a reading?' asked Probert.

'198, and the time is 10.20 p.m.,' responded Jowett, from beside the galvanometer. He turned to face Miss Crush. 'Don't you have something to tell us, madam?'

She gave a start that jerked her jet-earrings into glittering movement. 'Oh good gracious me! What do you wish me to say?'

'Merely what you said at this moment on Saturday evening – that you have reason to suspect that a spirit is abroad in the room, or words to that effect.'

'Did I really say such a thing?' asked Miss Crush.

'You detected a presence,' whispered Alice.

'Oh, my stars and garters! Yes, I did!' Miss Crush held up her forefinger. 'I divine a presence. We have a visitor with us.'

'And I can feel my hair being stroked,' said Alice, whose memory was more reliable.

'Wasn't this the moment when we heard the footsteps from behind the curtain?' asked Strathmore.

'It is all arranged,' said Jowett. 'Please behave exactly as you did on Saturday.'

A log subsided in the grate. There was a whimper from Miss Crush.

'Do you have your *sal volatile* with you, madam?' Probert inquired.

'In my hand, Doctor, in my hand.'

'The galvanometer is quite steady,' announced Jowett by way of reassurance.

202

Then they heard the door in the study open and the unmistakable sound of footsteps starting across the room and just as quickly returning.

'It's a bloody liberty,' called Cribb's voice, from behind the curtain.

'Shall I go to him?' asked Probert.

'No,' said Strathmore. 'If you remember, you asked me to go to the curtain first.'

'Please do so,' said Jowett.

Strathmore advanced to the curtain and opened a gap wide enough to peer through. 'Is everything in order?'

'No it ain't,' said Cribb's voice. 'Ask Dr Probert to come through.'

'Remember to kick over the bowl of water, Papa,' Alice helpfully advised.

Probert played his part with less zest than he had on Saturday, but everyone heard the bowl of salt solution being overturned, followed by his appeal for candles. Jowett lighted two and led the others through to where Cribb was seated.

'What the bleeding hell—' began Cribb.

'Very well, Sergeant,' interposed Jowett. 'We can afford to omit the unparliamentary language. Ladies present, you know. Is everything in order so far?'

'Yes, sir. The professor entered on cue and went out again.'

'Very good. Dr Probert, has Captain Nye gone downstairs to turn off the current?'

'He has, Inspector.'

'Splendid. What happened at this stage, then?'

'We tried to pacify the medium,' said Probert.

'So we did. Do you consider yourself pacified, Cribb?'

'Yes, sir.'

'And ready to die – in simulation, of course?'

'Yes, sir.'

'Stout fellow! Ah, I can hear Captain Nye approaching. Kindly ask him to go downstairs again and restore the electricity, will you, Miss Probert? I believe I returned to my galvanometer at this point in the proceedings.' Jowett was sounding increasingly like a host determined to inflict party games on unconvivial guests. He left the others standing woodenly round the chair and bustled through the curtain. 'Capital!' he presently announced. 'I have a reading of 195. We now commence the last phase of the exercise, ladies and gentlemen. Take your places, please.'

They filed silently through to the library, leaving Cribb to his simulated fate.

'I have a reading of 200 divisions, Mr Strathmore,' said Jowett, when everyone was seated.

Strathmore's co-operation in the reconstruction had not extended to copying the readings into a notebook, but he nodded, since his name had been mentioned.

It was the last movement in the library for an appreciable time, except for the flickering of the fire. Even Jowett had succumbed to the tension now, and was standing by the galvanometer with his hands locked tightly behind his back. Alice, on the edge of her chair, was poised to give support to Miss Crush, who was holding her bottle of *sal volatile* six inches from her nose. Somewhere in the house a grandfather clock chimed the half-hour.

'Half past ten. The needle is at 196, a slight drop, I think,' Jowett observed.

'Something is moving somewhere. I know it,' said Miss Crush.

'Steady, madam!' growled Probert.

'That man behind the curtain is a sensitive,' she insisted. 'Dear God, the room is getting colder! What is it, Captain Nye, what is it?'

Nye, apparently unwilling or unable to respond, lifted his arm to point ahead of him. His eyes stood out like two half-crowns in a penny bazaar. They were focused on an object which had appeared between the two sections of the curtain. It was a white, moving hand.

'God preserve us!' cried Miss Crush, pushing the *sal volatile* against her nose.

The hand came further round the curtain, exposing a wrist and forearm, partially draped in white.

Captain Nye slumped over the table in a dead faint.

'The galvanometer reading is the same!' said Jowett. 'Look at the needle, Strathmore!'

But Strathmore, like the others, had eyes only for the apparition which was gliding clear of the curtain and into the library. Its face and hands were as pallid as the shroud-like garment which enveloped it, but Miss Crush's perceptions had been sharpened by the *sal volatile*. 'I recognize it!' she said. 'Look at the nose and side-whiskers. It is the spirit of that poor man Cribb, passing through on its way to purgatory. The chair has taken him from us, as it did poor Peter.'

'Not so, madam!' said Jowett, in a dramatic intervention worthy to rank with anything Irving ever did on the boards of the Lyceum. 'That will do, Sergeant.'

The figure halted.

'Dear God!' exclaimed Miss Crush. 'It still obeys commands, poor, hapless thing. It has not yet freed itself from its mortal obligations.'

205

'I'm afraid not, ma'am,' said Cribb's voice. 'You can't give up the Force as easy as that.' He wiped some talcum powder away from his lips with the sleeve of his nightshirt. 'I seem to have alarmed Captain Nye, sir.'

'Not only Captain Nye,' said Probert. 'What the devil is this charade all about, Inspector?'

Jowett was quite unperturbed. 'I shall tell you, Doctor. I arranged this as a demonstration. This evening you have seen what Peter Brand intended you to see on Saturday evening: the apparent manifestation of a spirit. After his death we discovered that he was wearing a full-length nightshirt like this one of Cribb's under his outer clothes. In the pocket was a small bag of talcum powder for application to the face and hands, to give the ghostly pallor, you understand. It sounds like a parlour game, I admit, but in the uneven light of a fire and before sitters who have already witnessed other phenomena, it could, I believe, carry some conviction. Even Cribb's unrehearsed performance tonight seems to have impressed some of you. Are you feeling better, Captain Nye?'

'Perfectly well,' retorted the captain over the bottle of *sal volatile*. 'Haven't had enough sleep lately.'

Alice was frowning at what Jowett had said. 'But if Peter Brand had dressed up – or, rather, undressed – like this, and left the chair, we should have known as soon as he took his hands away from the brass handles and broke the electrical circuit.'

'A valid observation, Miss Probert,' said Jowett, obviously relishing his role as unraveller of the mystery. 'Won't you kindly come over here and examine the galvanometer?'

The invitation was to Alice, but she was joined there by everyone else.

'Damn it, the confounded thing is still registering 196!' said Probert. 'There's something amiss.'

'There must be somebody else in the chair!' said Alice. 'An accomplice! That large policeman with the beard.'

'No, Miss Probert. You are quite mistaken,' said Jowett. 'Come and see for yourself.' He walked to the curtains and drew them emphatically apart.

There was nobody seated in the chair. Stretched between the handles was a white handkerchief.

'What's a blasted wipe doing there?' demanded Probert.

'Standing in for Sergeant Cribb, Doctor,' said Jowett. 'You wouldn't think a pocket handkerchief could stretch that far until you held it by opposite corners and saw the length of it. It tucks in nicely where the handle is screwed to the wood.'

'A handkerchief won't conduct electricity,' said Probert.

'Ah, but a wet one will,' said Jowett. 'And this one's nice and wet from mopping up the water I spilt when I knocked over the flowers. You did a good job there, Cribb, and very naturally as well.'

'Thank you, sir,' said Cribb.

'We take no credit for the idea,' Jowett went on, having conceded Cribb as much gratification as was good for him. 'That was Brand's. And he was clever enough to knock the chrysanthemums over with an orange – unless somebody put out a hand in the dark to assist the operation, and I suppose we'll never know that for certain. However, he got his handkerchief saturated in a perfectly accountable way, by very decently agreeing to wipe up the water himself. He then replaced it in his pocket and took his place in the chair.'

'How would he remove the handkerchief from his pocket when he was holding the handles?' asked Strathmore.

'That is easier than it might appear. He could not take his hands off the handles without breaking the current, it is true, but that still permitted him a considerable amount of movement with the rest of his body. It would not be difficult to bring the right pocket into a position where the thumb of the right hand could hook out the handkerchief. So long as the palm of that hand remained firmly on the handle he could use the fingers to fasten the end of the handkerchief as you see it here. He then had only to pick up the loose end in his teeth and transfer it to the left hand, and secure it to the handle. The contact would thus be unbroken, and he could leave the chair by passing the upper half of his body under the handkerchief. Sergeant Cribb is not a contortionist, but he seems to have achieved this feat without trouble. Is that so, Sergeant?'

'Yes, sir.'

'The rest you have seen for yourselves,' said Jowett, spreading out his hands.

Nye was frowning. 'We've seen what the poor beggar planned to do, but you haven't shown us how he was killed.'

'That's a different question, Captain, but you shall have the answer if you would oblige me by going downstairs to turn off the electricity again – for the last time, I do assure you. And Cribb, Constable Thackeray is waiting outside the door, I believe. Ask him to step inside, will you?'

'Dressed like this, sir?' said Cribb, frowning.

'If you please. After that you may step behind the curtain and put on your normal clothes. I need Thackeray to take the part of the corpse. He is experienced in the role, you told me.'

'That's right, sir. He's a natural in the part.' Cribb paused,

208

remembering something. 'Might I make one small request, sir? I'd like to put my jacket and trousers on again first. I wouldn't care for Thackeray to see me like this. Not good for discipline.'

'Really?' Jowett eyed the nightshirt speculatively. 'I suppose not. Be quick then. We can't keep everyone here till midnight, you know.'

'I trust that it will not distress anybody if I ask the constable to adopt the position in which we found Mr Brand,' Jowett resumed, after Thackeray had entered, wearing an eye-shade.

There was no dissent, although Captain Nye was staring fixedly at Thackeray, frowning and inclining his head slightly to one side and then to the other. The constable was glad to have a reason to turn his back, sit in the chair, and give his impression of an electrocuted corpse. When he was propped stiffly against the left-hand side, he explained between his teeth, 'By rights my hair should be standing on end, sir.'

'This is quite realistic enough for our purposes,' said Jowett. 'Now, ladies and gentlemen, I want you to notice most particularly the position of the left hand which is not gripping the handle as one might expect. In electrocution the muscles contract and the hand takes an even stronger grip on anything it is holding. But what has happened here? The left arm dangles over the left arm of the chair. You may relax, Thackeray.'

'Thank you, sir.'

'So we asked ourselves why the body should have been in this position,' Jowett continued.

'Perhaps the handkerchief had fallen on the floor and he was reaching to pick it up,' suggested Alice. 'He could grip the left handle with his teeth to maintain the electrical contact.'

'That's clever thinking, Miss Probert,' said Jowett, 'but it isn't quite consistent with the facts. Mr Brand couldn't have received a shock of four hundred volts by doing what you say.'

'The only way he'd get a shock like that is by touching the main cable,' said Probert, 'but it's out of reach behind the chair. Anyone can see that.'

'Quite right, Doctor,' said Jowett. 'But let us suppose that instead of the damp handkerchief lying on the floor here, as your daughter suggested, it was here.' He pointed to the transformer. 'Let us suppose that one end of it was attached to the positive terminal on the main side of the box. What do you suppose would happen if the medium reached out with his hand to recover the hand-kerchief – which we have seen was essential to his purpose?'

'He would die the moment he touched it,' said Strathmore, 'but are you really asking us to believe that the handkerchief fell from the chair and somehow landed three feet behind it with one corner attached to the positive terminal?'

'No, sir,' said Jowett. 'It was placed there as a deliberate act.'

'But that would be murder!' said Nye.

'It was.'

'Wait a moment, gentlemen!' said Alice. 'I think you have forgotten something. If this theory is to be believed, we should have found the handkerchief attached to the trans-former when we discovered poor Mr Brand in here.'

'We should indeed,' agreed Jowett, 'but it was not there

or anywhere in sight. And the interesting thing is that there was no handkerchief among the list of possessions found on Mr Brand's body. We are quite sure that he had one, because he mopped up the chrysanthemum-water with it. There is only one explanation possible, and that is that it was picked up by one of you – after Mr Brand had been murdered.'

The drift of Jowett's thesis must have been increasingly obvious, but this conclusion still had the effect of stunning everybody. Miss Crush gasped with such force that it was difficult to tell how many smaller intakes of breath occurred at that precise moment.

Probert was the first to respond. 'Before anyone begins to make assertions about present company, I think you ought to make it absolutely clear, Inspector, that this is an engaging theory without any basis of evidence. I'm no lawyer, but I know enough about the workings of the courts to point out that the Attorney-General himself couldn't prove what you're saying without a witness to the facts. Let's see if we have one, shall we? I ask you, ladies and gentlemen, did any one of you see a handkerchief attached to the transformer as Inspector Jowett has postulated?' He looked at each person in turn, with eyebrows speculatively raised. 'You see? Not one witness. You can't even produce the confounded handkerchief! It's like trying to prove a poisoning without the arsenic.'

This was clearly not the response Jowett had expected. He frowned, cleared his throat and rubbed the side of his face. He had the look of a conjurer who had waved his wand and been unable to produce a rabbit from his hat.

'It's plausible, I'll grant you that,' Probert continued, pressing home his advantage, 'but you've got no proof.

There's nothing on earth to show that a wet handkerchief was ever tied to that transformer.'

Sergeant Cribb, who had been a bystander in all this, put his hand in his pocket. The movement, slight as it was, drew the attention from Jowett's bleak countenance. Cribb withdrew his pocket-book, turned the pages methodically, found his place and opened it. 'You require some proof, sir? I found these on the carpet beside the transformer.' He tipped two thin wisps, no more than an inch in length, into his palm and held them out for inspection.

'What the devil are they?' asked Probert.

'Chrysanthemum petals,' said Cribb. 'They must have been picked up by Brand's handkerchief when he wiped the mantelpiece dry. Tiny things, ain't they? I don't suppose you noticed them on Saturday when you picked the hand-kerchief up and put it in your pocket after Peter Brand's death, Doctor.'

15

Now for it then! Will you believe me, though?
You've heard what I confess; I don't unsay
A single word . . .

'Inspector Jowett, said Probert, 'do I take it that this subordinate of yours has your authority to level this outrageous accusation at me in my own house, in the presence of my daughter and guests?'

'Do you deny it, sir?' asked Cribb, before Jowett could respond.

'Deuced impertinence!' exclaimed Captain Nye. 'Dr Probert is a member of the Royal Society. I don't care for this man's manner, Inspector, any more than I care for the look of this other person with the patch over his eye. If you hadn't told us he was a policeman, I'd stake my reputation that I met him recently in very disagreeable circumstances. I don't know what the police are coming to when men of this class are brought into private residences to fling abuse at decent people.'

'Sergeant Cribb and Constable Thackeray are two of the most experienced detectives in Scotland Yard,' said Jowett. It should have been a splendid affirmation of confidence. The pity was that Jowett's emphasis made it sound like an admission that the Force had problems over recruitment. 'I'm sure no insult was intended, gentlemen.'

Cribb confirmed this with a nod and added mildly, 'I simply stated a fact.'

The effect of this was to give an extra twist to the curl of Captain Nye's lips. Not content with resembling a camel, he began to make sounds like one.

'Please, William,' Alice appealed to him. 'For everyone's sake, keep calm.'

Inspector Jowett, too, was anxious to avoid a scene. He leaned towards Cribb. 'It might be wise if you withdrew, Sergeant.'

It had been intended as a confidential remark, but Probert was quick to show that he had heard it. 'No, no, there is no need for that. The sergeant has obviously made a mistake and must accept my word for it. The incident is closed.'

'Not entirely,' said Strathmore, with the unsparing persistence of a seeker after truth. 'If the statement has no basis of fact, you are entitled to an apology at the very least. The officer seems confident of his facts. Let him substantiate them. Tell us, Sergeant, what reason do you have for stating that Dr Probert picked up the handkerchief?'

Cribb glanced towards Jowett, who looked uneasy, but nodded his consent to proceed.

'Well, sir, you will recollect that when we pulled aside the curtain on Saturday night and found Mr Brand dead, we were unprepared for the sight that confronted us.'

'Unprepared!' cried Alice. 'That's an understatement if ever I heard one!'

'If you say so, miss,' said Cribb. 'What matters is that our eyes fastened on Mr Brand. We failed to notice the handkerchief attached to the transformer. Observation is my job, but I don't mind admitting that I was so taken up with the appearance of the deceased that I didn't look behind the chair. It's only on a second look that you notice a thing like that, but when I came to take a second look there wasn't any handkerchief there.'

'Is that to be wondered at?' said Probert. 'You went upstairs in pursuit of Professor Quayle. By the time you and the inspector came back into the library we had moved the body out of the chair. Any one of us could have picked up the blasted handkerchief.'

'That's right, sir. One's the word. It was a solitary action. There wasn't anybody else to see you pick it up or we'd have heard about it before now.'

'But why, Papa?' said Alice. 'Why do you keep saying *he* was the one?'

'I'll explain, miss. First I want you to answer me a question. After the curtain was pulled back, and you saw what had happened, can you remember what you did?'

'Of course. I attended to Miss Crush. She had started forward as if to touch Mr Brand. Papa shouted a warning, you restrained her and she fainted. I then helped you move her to the couch and I did the things one is recommended to do in cases of collapse, such as loosening her clothes.'

'Thank you, my dear,' said Miss Crush, putting her hand on Alice's arm.

'And you, sir,' Cribb went on, turning to Nye. 'What did you do at this time?'

The captain was clearly unhappy about answering questions from an officer of non-commissioned rank, so he gazed imperiously into the distance as he spoke. 'What did I do? What I seem to have been doing all the week.

I went downstairs at the double to turn off the blasted electricity.'

'How long did it take you to get downstairs?'

'I wouldn't know. Not more than a few seconds, I should think. As soon as I had switched the thing off, I shouted up to your inspector.'

'Ah, yes.' Cribb turned to Jowett. 'You were waiting at the top of the stairs, I believe, sir?'

'That is correct,' Jowett confirmed. 'In turn, I shouted to Dr Probert that the current was off.'

'Thank you, sir.' Cribb addressed Strathmore: 'And where were you, sir, when Inspector Jowett shouted that the electricity was turned off?'

'I was beside the fireplace in the library,' answered Strathmore. 'Dr Probert had asked me to fetch candles, if you remember, as we had no light in the study.'

'I do, sir,' said Cribb with a nod. 'So we have a clear picture of the situation, ladies and gentlemen. When word came that the electricity was off, Mr Stathmore was in the library lighting the candles. Miss Crush had fainted, and Miss Probert and I were attending to her. Captain Nye was in the basement and Inspector Jowett was at the head of the basement stairs. The only person beside this chair was you, Dr Probert, and that was when you must have picked up the handkerchief and pocketed it. Immediately after, Mr Strathmore brought the candles and then you could not have done it unnoticed, and nor could anyone else.'

There were a few seconds' silence as people took in the significance of Cribb's argument. Then eyes began to turn in Probert's direction, as if by general consent it was his turn to justify himself.

Alice was the last to face him and the first to speak. 'Papa, this isn't true, is it?'

Probert took a handkerchief from his pocket, apparently without appreciating the effect this normally innocent action would have on people. He blew his nose and Miss Crush jerked with the shock. 'Very well,' he said. 'You shall have the truth. I *did* pick up the handkerchief, just as you say, Sergeant.'

'No!' said Alice, her face drained of colour. 'By why, Papa, why?'

'That should be clear to everyone,' said Probert. 'I saw the man lying dead in front of me and there was the chance of avoiding the odium of a murder investigation in my house, so as soon as the current was switched off I pocketed the handkerchief. I burned it later. That's all it was.'

'I don't think so, sir,' said Cribb.

'Are you contradicting me?' said Probert, more as an inquiry than a challenge.

'We've got to establish the truth, sir. You say you didn't want a murder investigated in your house, but what made you think of murder? A pocket handkerchief isn't usually classed as a lethal weapon.'

'It was attached to the positive terminal of the trans-former,' Probert pointed out.

'I don't doubt that, sir. What I doubt is whether that should have suggested murder to you at that particular moment. It would still look more like an accident to me. But perhaps murder was in your mind.'

'Father!' said Alice. 'He has no right to speak to you like that!'

Dr Probert was looking too uncomfortable by far to take issue over Sergeant Cribb's rights. He silenced Alice by

217

limply waving his hand. 'Sergeant, I am not sure how it has happened, but you seem to have me against a wall. If you want my full confession to the murder of Peter Brand I am ready to give it to you, but I should prefer not to do so in front of these people who are my friends and family.'

'Father!' cried Alice. 'It can't be true! It isn't true!' She ran to Probert and caught him by the arm. 'Say it isn't true!'

'Go upstairs to your mother and tell her as gently as you can,' said Probert.

Cribb put up his hand. 'Before you do that, miss, there's something you must say to your father. I want you to tell him in your own words – so that he can see you're telling the gospel truth – that you are not the murderer of Peter Brand.'

'Are you serious?' said Alice.

'Never more serious, miss. Your father believes you arranged to kill Brand to silence him over a certain matter arising from your visits to a hat-shop. On the night of the seance he couldn't fail to notice that you were collaborating with Brand by tapping the table and claiming to be touched by spirit hands. He concluded that you were being black-mailed by the medium, and when the body was discovered he assumed you were responsible. He picked up the hand-kerchief, thinking to divert suspicion from you. Unless you can dissuade him, he is now about to make a false confes-sion in order, as he believes, to save you from the hangman's rope. It's an admirable gesture, and I'm sure we all applaud him for it, but I hope you can convince him that it isn't necessary. Constable Thackeray here doesn't take kindly to copying out statements only to tear 'em up.'

Alice had listened with an expression of disbelief growing

into astonishment and finally awe. She shook her head slowly, temporarily unable to find words.

Miss Crush filled the breach. 'It would be rather extravagant to murder somebody because of something that happened in a hat-shop.'

'It's utterly incredible!' said Alice. 'Papa, you didn't really believe this, did you? I agreed to help Peter Brand in the seance to stop him making mischief in the family, but I've explained all that. You *know* why I changed my clothes there.' She gripped her father's arm and studied his face, searching for some sign of comprehension.

He avoided her eyes. 'I know that you have accounted for your behaviour, Alice, but that conversation took place on Sunday, remember. On Saturday night, when I saw him dead, I could only think that you must have arranged it in some way. You have always been a strong-headed girl. I saw the handkerchief and I understood how it had been done.'

'But Peter Brand didn't bother me to that extent!' cried Alice. 'It was to protect *you* from embarrassment that I did what he asked me to do at the seance. It was no reason for killing him. If I had felt strongly about it I should have asked William to give him a thrashing.'

'By Jove, yes!' said Nye enthusiastically. 'The bounder deserved it. It's a damned shame he isn't around now, or I'd alter the shape of his nose.'

'Don't provoke the departed,' said Miss Crush, wagging her finger at Nye.

'Papa,' said Alice. 'You *do* see how ridiculous your suspicions were, don't you?'

'I need to sit down,' said Dr Probert. 'Constable, do you mind?'

Thackeray sprang out of the chair with surprising agility

for a corpse and slipped to the back of the group, well out of Captain Nye's range. Probert took his place. 'Yes, my dear. I believe you. But *somebody* must have put that handkerchief there, and for a good reason.'

Cribb caught Jowett's eye. 'Would you like to explain, sir?'

'Now that you have started, you might as well continue, Sergeant,' said the inspector, as if the whole thing bored him.

'If you insist, sir. Well, we know how Peter Brand came to be electrocuted and we know that somebody must have arranged it. A handkerchief doesn't fall two feet behind a chair and wind itself around a terminal. We can also tell when it was done.'

'It must have been after the first interruption,' said Strathmore. 'We all went into the study to calm Brand down after the footsteps – which we now know to have been Professor Quayle's – had broken his concentration. That was when the handkerchief must have been put down. When we resumed, we had normal readings on the galvanometer for a few minutes, and then he must have realized that the handkerchief was on the floor and reached out to pick it up, with fatal consequences.'

'Thank you, sir,' said Cribb. 'That's exactly how I see it.'

Strathmore smiled. 'I believe I remarked before that, as investigators, we are two of a kind, Sergeant.'

'So you did, sir. There it is, then. Scotland Yard and the Life After Death Society agree how and when the crime was committed. And once you've got the "how" and the "when", the "who" is easier to find.'

'But any one of us could have attached the end of the handkerchief to the transformer,' said Alice. 'It would not have been a conspicuous action by candlelight, and in so much confusion.'

'Quite right, miss. So we have to find a way to determine who is most likely to have done it.'

'A motive,' said Captain Nye.

'That's important, yes, sir, but I had something else in mind. Motives are helpful, but when everybody has a motive you can't rely on them alone.'

'What do you mean – "everybody"?' said Nye. 'I'd like to know what motive you could ascribe to me. I had no interest in doing away with that nasty little table-tapping mountebank.'

'It's not necessary to go into the question of motives,' Cribb firmly explained.

'Quite right too,' concurred Miss Crush.

'I expect he thought you might have been moved to do it on my account,' Alice suggested to her fiancé.

Nye beamed. 'That hadn't occurred to me.'

'And you do have an ungovernable temper,' added Alice.

'Leaving motives aside, then,' Cribb quickly said, 'it's part of a detective's job to make deductions from the circumstances of a crime. The circumstances here are quite exceptional, because they show that the murder depended on events nobody could have predicted. For Peter Brand to die by electrocution there had to be a wet handkerchief which he would be obliged to reach for, and the purpose of that handkerchief was a secret known only to Brand; there had to be a damp patch on the carpet where his feet made contact, so that the current would pass through his body to earth – and that, in case you have forgotten, was provided by Dr Probert accidentally kicking over the bowl of salt solution; and there had to be an opportunity to put the handkerchief in position – and that only came about by chance because of Professor Quayle's interruption, when Brand stopped the seance and would not continue until we calmed him down.'

'It begins to sound more like an accident than a deliberate act,' said Strathmore.

'No, sir. We can't get away from the fact that somebody put the handkerchief in a position where it was certain to kill Brand when he touched it. What we can say with certainty is that the action wasn't planned from the beginning of the evening.'

'In legal parlance, it was not done with malice aforethought,' said Strathmore.

'I didn't say that, sir.'

'Well, it was not premeditated.'

'I prefer to say that it was improvised,' said Cribb. 'The murderer made use of circumstances that did not occur by his or her design. That, you see, tells us a lot about the nature of the crime. It was the subject of a quick decision, a decision that was possible only in that interval after the professor's interruption. Only then did the circumstances make a murder conceivable at all.'

'Something must have happened,' said Alice. 'Mr Brand must have said or done something that drove one of us to a sudden act of murder. What could that have been?'

'I'll tell you, miss. It was the sight of Peter Brand sitting in the chair with the handkerchief stretched between the handles. It showed that Brand was no more than a clever sharp, you see.'

'But I don't see, Sergeant. None of us saw what you describe. We had no idea that he was planning such a deception until you demonstrated it this evening.'

'I must correct you, miss. One of you did see it. When Brand called out after the interruption, somebody went to the curtain and looked through.'

'Strathmore!' said Probert. 'But he claimed he couldn't see a damned thing.'

'Take my word for it, sir. There was enough light when Mr Strathmore pulled aside the curtain to see a white handkerchief stretched between those chair-arms. That was why he was so particular in the reconstruction this evening about being the one to look through. He had to find out for himself whether I knew what he had seen last Saturday.'

Cribb turned to Strathmore. 'You don't deny it, do you, sir?'

Strathmore avoided the question. 'That's a slender thread to support a charge of murder, Sergeant.'

'There's more than that, sir. There's the question of your sudden change of attitude towards Brand. Before the murder you were quite ready to believe that your twelve years of searching for a genuine materializing medium were at an end. You were talking of your paper on the subject being read by scientists the world over – and who can blame you? How could you have known that three other people were assisting Brand in producing his phenomena? It was inconceivable that people like the Proberts and Miss Crush could be persuaded to collaborate with an imposter. No, every indication suggested that you had achieved the ultimate purpose of your Society – to prove the existence of life after death in scientifically controlled conditions. In short, sir, you were duped, and the first moment you realized it was when you looked through that curtain, before Brand had the wit to get the handkerchief back into his pocket. During those minutes of confusion when everyone was trying to account for what had happened, you removed the hand-kerchief from Brand's pocket.'

'It was partially on view, I remember,' contributed Jowett.

'Anyway, it was no difficult matter to gain possession of it while you were re-connecting wires,' said Cribb. 'Once the current was turned off, you twisted the end round the terminal on the transformer and left Brand to his fate.'

Strathmore had listened with extraordinary calm. 'If he had been a genuine medium,' he said, 'he would not have needed to touch the handkerchief. My action put him to the test. Is that really murder?'

'That's a question a court of law might argue over, sir, but it's my duty to charge you with murder, I'm sure of that.'

Strathmore produced a handkerchief and polished his monocle methodically. 'I should like to hear the rest of your case, Sergeant. What made you certain that I was responsible for Brand's death? It seems to me you might equally have charged Dr Probert.'

'Go to the devil!' said Probert.

'I probably shall, but it would interest me to know why you're not going in my place.'

'I'll tell you,' said Cribb, whose respect for Strathmore was growing. A man who could face a charge of murder with dignity was not wholly to be despised. 'If Dr Probert had killed Brand it would have been for a different reason, a reason he knew about on Friday evening, the night before the seance. He had *time* to plan a murder. He wouldn't have left it to chance. He could have built a fault into the transformer which would have killed Brand and been accepted as an accident. He had no need to use a handkerchief.'

'He pocketed it afterwards,' said Strathmore.

'He did – and that, more than anything, convinced me that he hadn't put it there in the first place. It was the action of a man in a panic, a man who had just seen it there and realized its purpose. He put it in his pocket thinking to protect his daughter. That must have made things difficult for you, Mr Strathmore, because you intended the handkerchief to be found, didn't you?'

'The whole thing might have been passed off as an accident,' Strathmore agreed.

'Yes, but you had another reason for wanting it to be found,' said Cribb. 'You wanted the world to know that Brand had cheated, and the handkerchief was going to be the proof of that. Instead, you were put into the position of calling him a fraud without any proof at all. Even after he was dead, you couldn't bear to let anyone believe he might have been genuine, and you made your change of opinion very clear. I remember that Captain Nye commented upon it at the time.'

'Quite right,' said Nye. 'It was a damned quick turn about, and I said so. You also made some very dubious remarks about my fiancée's part in the seance.'

'With good foundation, I gather,' said Strathmore. He ignored Nye's spluttering reaction to this, and faced Cribb. 'Thank you for the explanation, Sergeant. I can see that my mistake was that I behaved unscientifically. I made an assertion which I knew to be true before I could support it with a demonstrable proof. I should have waited for the *post mortem* to have shown incontestably that Brand was a cheat. I was unscientific, but I can at least claim to have acted in a way consistent with truth, as I have always tried to do in my years of searching for the evidence of life after death. I cannot say the same of all my fellow-searchers.' He faced Cribb steadily and at that moment looked the least guilt-ridden of all Dr Probert's guests. 'Do you require a statement at this stage, Sergeant, or will you take it at the police station?'

'Will he hang?' Thackeray asked Cribb in the small hours of the morning after the door was closed on Strathmore's cell in Richmond police station.

'Difficult to say. It's got the makings of a classic trial. Everything should hinge on the question of intent. If you read the statement through, you'll notice that he gave a very clear account of his actions, but said nothing of motives. He's a very knowing card, is our Mr Strathmore, and he'll stand up well in the dock. Yes, I think a good defence counsel has the chance of winning an acquittal. We've done our job. It's a matter for the lawyers now.'

'The press will have a field-day when Miss Crush and Alice Probert go into the witness-box. By the way, Sarge, the Proberts still don't seem to know the real reason why Alice kept visiting the hat-shop. They don't know what I saw through the window at Maids of Honour Row, and nor does Captain Nye.'

'Better all round if they never find out,' said Cribb. 'It won't affect the outcome of the case. No need to upset Captain Nye any more. He's a great bore, I know, but he'll make a staunch husband for Alice Probert, and she needs an anchorage. Why, if you think back on it, you probably imagined it all, swaying up there on a trellis, trying to see through a first-floor window.'

'I don't imagine things,' protested Thackeray. 'I had a perfectly clear view. The sun was shining into the room. I've always been an accurate observer.'

Cribb shook his head slowly. 'Thackeray, it's very late, I know, and this has been a hard week. I would have thought it might have taught you that you can't believe everything your eyes tell you, but as it obviously hasn't, I must tell you about an item of police equipment that you may not know you have. It's your blind eye, and it's just as important as your bullseye lamp or your truncheon. Knowing when to use it is the test of a successful bobby.' He put his hand on Thackeray's shoulder. 'When we met the Proberts they were a disunited family, but I think they've learned a little. Let's turn that blind eye and leave 'em the chance of finding a spot of harmony.'

'If you say so, Sarge,' said Thackeray, 'but I wouldn't put the chance very high.'

'Why not?'

'There was something I noticed earlier this evening, but I didn't report it to you. I was – er – using my blind eye.'

'Oh?' Cribb gave Thackeray a long look.

'Yes, I was waiting in the corridor outside the library while you were reconstructing the seance, if you remember. I didn't hear much of what was going on, but I saw Professor Quayle tiptoe into the study and come out again.'

'Quite right,' said Cribb. 'That was what he did on Saturday. He played his part convincingly.'

'That's a fact, Sarge. He even had a bottle of gin in his pocket. After he came out of the study he made his way upstairs to Mrs Probert's room.'

'That wasn't strictly necessary to the investigation,' said Cribb, 'but I suppose he was retracing the movements he made on Saturday.'

'That's what I supposed, Sarge, and I thought I'd better

try to play your part and follow him upstairs. And that was when I had to turn my blind eye.'

'What do you mean?'

'Well, I think Mrs Probert didn't understand what he was coming up the stairs for. She opened her door and instead of throwing her book of sermons at him she pulled him inside and closed it. I shouldn't think there will be much of that gin left by now, and I don't give much chance of harmony on Richmond Hill tonight when Dr Probert finds out.'

Cribb smiled. 'I wouldn't lose any sleep over that, Thackeray. The last I saw of Dr Probert, he was inviting Miss Crush to take a look at his Etty.'

'Well, I hope she knows how to turn a blind eye,' said Thackeray.

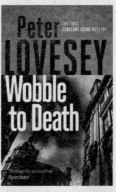

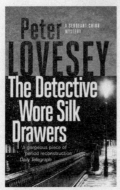
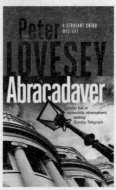

Discover Sergeant Cribb

'Lovesey has a special flair for re-creating Victorian
England with to-the-manner-born wit'
Saturday Review

'Sinister fun in splendidly atmospheric setting'
Sunday Telegraph

'Delightful Victorian mysteries . . . [A] fine picture of vice,
good mystery plotting, and fun'
San Francisco Chronicle

Discover Sergeant Cribb

**The very first Peter Diamond mystery,
and Anthony Award-winning novel, from
the superb Peter Lovesey**

A woman's naked body is found floating in the weeds
of a lake near Bath, by an elderly woman walking her
Siamese cats. No one comes forward to identify her,
and no murder weapon is found, but sleuthing is
Superintendent Peter Diamond's speciality. A genuine
gumshoe, practising door-stopping and deduction:
he is the last detective.

Struggling with office politics and a bizarre cast of
suspects, Diamond strikes out on his own, even when
Forensics think they have the culprit. Eventually, despite
disastrous personal consequences, and amongst Bath's
rambling buildings and formidable history, the last
detective exposes the uncomfortable truth . . .

*

'A bravura performance from a veteran showman:
slyly paced, marbled with surprise and, in the end,
strangely affecting'
New York Times Book Review